For Mum

The Hawthorn Cross

&

other

Antiques Ghost Stories

by

Michael Baggott

Introduction.

To every Antiques Dealer an object has its very own unique story. Beyond its design and manufacture, the tale of its ownership and long journey around the globe and down through the centuries. These are some simple imagined tales of some of those Antiques in hopefully the best tradition of the Antiquarian Ghost Story.

It's as well to remember not all Antiques are possessed of supernatural powers or evil spirits,

just most of them.

Contents

The King's Mirror

Ed had gotten up early to get to the fair at Stafford, it was bitterly cold and he'd even had to run around de-icing the car before setting off. There had been a smattering of snow which covered patches of black ice on the road, he nearly twice skidded off into a waiting ditch and only persevered as it was the day after Christmas and he was nearly stir crazy with Paul, his flat mate, in full chaotic residence, playing loud dance music and smoking weed all night.

When he finally arrived a bit later than he'd anticipated, going so slowly down the worst of winding frosted hedgerowed lanes, with its unfriendly brittle uncut twigs sticking out like fingers waiting to scratch the paint work of his beaten up Volvo as he passed. Hardly anyone had bothered to turn up, put off by the weather.

"What a waste" he muttered to himself, all too aware of the price of petrol and the lack of money in his wallet. He got a quick polystyrene cup of tea from the outside catering van which tasted as thin and weak as washing up water and set off back home to Birmingham, hoping the roads would be a bit kinder now the Sun was fully up.

He started off the way he came but, as he was about to join the main road back, a small unmanned road works, that he hadn't seen coming, blocked the way and a yellow "Diversion" sign pointed him down a single track road to his right. He turned onto its narrow and uneven surface with the car lurching up and down over the pot holes, he prayed there wouldn't be a

1

morning farmer in his tractor coming the other way forcing him to reverse, happily there wasn't.

After about half a mile the road broadened out and he could see he was driving alongside an old brick wall, the type that usually bordered a Georgian estate, though quickly checking he couldn't see one marked on his AA road map. As he came to the end of the road it split in a T junction left and right, the right turn had another yellow "Diversion" to follow but the left had a homemade "Carboot sale and fate", with the day's date pointing to the left. What would be the harm he thought in just having a quick look?

Following the left turn for a few hundred yards, continuing along the old estate wall he came to a high wrought iron gate, reminiscent of the work of Jean Tijou, "impressive" he thought, it was open and he proceeded in along a gravel drive. In front of him was a slightly small but derelict Tudor house rather like a small Wightwick Manor though the black and white of the timber and walls had faded to a bleached oak and a dirty brown. To his right was a large lawn, probably once a knot garden and on it were a few, perhaps no more than two dozen parked vehicles with locals selling all manner of unwanted household rubbish. He parked and walked towards them.

A young girl in jeans and a several layer of thick fleece sat on a wooden chair before a melamine table at the entrance to the lawn and lifted her hand as she said "50p entrance, all to raise money for the Circle Trust" he paid and was offered a small printed leaflet, he could see the words "Charitable Donations" so immediately declined, much to her disappointment.

It was cold but bright and it seemed the crows from a nearby coppice had just woken up with a constant caw-cawing noise that anyone who has lived in the countryside will be all too familiar with.

He picked through boxes of tools and toys, some old books were on table tops along with DVD's and used electrical equipment, it was looking like a monumental waste of time. At the end of the last row it seemed to become a little quieter, not that Ed really noticed but the incessant noise of the crows had died down and the other people seemed slightly distant, he approached an old man by an oak, was it oak? table, it was covered with papers.

"You don't seem to have a car with you, bit odd for a Car boot?"

"No sir" replied a thick rural accent, possibly with a touch of Welsh, well we were near the borders, "I'm from the House, the Circle Trust you'll have seen the leaflets as you came in"

"Oh, yes, the leaflets" (the ones he'd dodged) "I haven't had chance to read..." he lied to spare himself any embarrassment.

The older man explained that the house, known as Skuggsby Hall (a corruption of the Old Norse 'Skuggsja') had been left derelict for a number of years and was currently the property of the local council, though they had left matters of the preservation and fundraising to a local Trust.

"The Circle Trust, why Circle?"

"Why don't you know you Sir?!" the older man exclaimed and pointed beyond the garden to a slope inclining upwards, a large shallow earth work with what looked like stones dotted around the top.

"That's the stone circle, been there they reckon for thousands of years. They're digging it up soon, people from the University, to see if there's anything there." He smiled, a not altogether easy smile, which had a tone of mischief and menace, but Ed had not noticed it, his interest was in the papers, some of them parchment that lay on the table before him.

"Where are these from? The Hall?"

He guessed right, anything still in the building and there wasn't much was to be sold for upkeep. He could hope for a Tudor backstool or a piece of Carolean stumpwork, but all he was going to get was a collection of rather mundane Estate Papers for the 18th and 19th century. His heart sank a little but he wanted at least to cover his petrol money for the day and the 50p it had cost to get in.

"What about this Sir?" The old man handed him a thick ledger with a leather bound spine and corners in quite reasonable order, a Georgian set of household accounts.

"Well it's not very interesting, but to help how much?"

He knew an academic collector at the University in Birmingham who liked household accounts, how much the footman was paid each quarter, what was the household expenditure of Coal, etc, so it was worth at least £80, maybe £100 on a good day"

"£15?" The old man replied. "Well, I could certainly go to £10 but that's my limit"

The old man nodded and grasped his hand to close the deal, it felt bitter cold even in the Sun.

Happy with his purchase Ed returned back to the flat via the Diversions, music was still playing loudly and his housemate was still, this late in the day, in a state of leisurely undress.

"Wotcha, had a good day?" said Paul as Ed struggled in with the ledger dropping it onto a nearby table covered mostly with old take-away cartons.

"Fair was rubbish, but I picked this old Ledger up at a Car boot in a nice out of the way old hall, Tudor I think, but run down. It wasn't on the map"

Paul, still part intoxicated, part stoned picked the Ledger up in a half comical manner, but his coordination was off and the joke turned sour as the book fell, with its full weight, half open onto the spine.

"You IDIOT!" shouted Ed, "You've only gone and torn the bloody binding!"

He was right. The book lay in nearly two pieces on the floor, the leather binding and covers pulled apart by the weight of the impact.

"I'm sorry" said Paul as he lurched forward to pick it up. "Stop" shouted Ed.

He peered down and could see the small corner of an illustrated page sticking out from between the binding, it had clearly been concealed.

"Just give me a hand to get it on the table, gently, GENTLY!"

The take-away cartons were swept immediately onto the floor and the book placed on it. Ed needed space to work. He got the thinnest pair of nail scissors he could find, a Stanley knife and some tweezers that one of Paul's numerous girlfriends had left in the bathroom. He drew up a chair and began to operate.

He cut as delicately as he could along the lines of the binding where the small illustrated document (clearly old) was protruding from. He snipped through the leather corners and spine with the scissors and used the tweezers to pry the two boards apart. At first they were reluctant to move but all of a sudden they gave way and three pieces of vellum dropped onto the table.

The first was a map which appeared to show where he had been earlier that day, The Hall but with a knot garden and some walls which were not there now, he'd have remembered. Then there was a path leading up the earthworks to the right of the house towards the stone circle and beyond that a small wood or coppice was marked. There appeared to be a faint red line tracing a path one to the other, then, in the woodland a small black square was drawn with some lettering around it he could not make out. A treasure map? Ed wondered.

The second was a squared piece of vellum completely plain save for a series of straight and angled lines running around the border of the back and front of the page and nothing else except for a finely drawn Crest on the reverse, surely of the owner, depicting the figure of an ancient Wodesman (a common enough device in early family heraldry) beside what appeared to be a mirror, with the initials "JS" in a beautiful gothic style hand beneath it.

The third was even more perplexing, a series of symbols in rows on a folded vellum which when fully opened ran to over four pages of A4, though again at the bottom were the initials "JS".

Any anger Ed had at Paul for ruining a domestic nineteenth century ledger had evaporated, here, he felt he may have Tudor documents, one illustrated, one clearly gibberish and one possibly an Elizabethan cypher. He could hardly contain his excitement, though he never gave a second thought to returning them back to the Circle Trust for the upkeep of Skuggsby Hall either.

Tomorrow he would take the cypher and the crested vellum (but NOT the map) to the University Professor he knew. He had in the past bought several antiquities (another sideline) from Ed and he was sure he would be able to cast some light upon them. The map though, that was something he'd keep as an ace in the hole for now, afterall who knew what it might point to?

Bright and early he made his way to the University Campus as he clutched the two precious finds on approaching the famous Birmingham clock tower. Professor John Blickstone was in his rooms and already prepared for the early visit.

"Hello Prof, how are you?" Some usual pleasantries were exchanged before Ed pulled out the much anticipated two documents from his bag and placed them before the eager academic.

"Hmm, Hmm" it was a usual sound when anyone is slightly confounded and surprised by what they're looking at, "Interesting, very interesting. Where did you get them from?"

"A small country auction" Ed lied, he did not want to reveal too much and was certain to not make mention of the map which accompanied them, "They were in a box of odds and ends"

"Well, you've done very well" replied the Professor. "They are definitely sixteenth century I'd say, can't be precise of course, maybe 1570's, 1580's"

This is the confirmation that Ed wanted to hear, though the scrap of square vellum with the Crest and lines upon it might be worth one or two hundred, a long sheet of cyphers would certainly run into the low thousands at least, more if he could actually understand what it said.

"Do you think you can tell what its about Prof?" Ed was trying to get as much free help as he could, besides he could see the old man was dying of curiosity.

"Well, I'm busy at the moment, but if you leave them with me for a while I'll have a go, show them to some colleagues, at the very least I should be able to tell you who the Crest belongs to."

"Ok, I'll leave them with you and call back in a couple of weeks"

Ed determined that he would return to Skuggsby Hall at the weekend and see if he could find out any more about its history, perhaps the Circle Trust could help, not that he wanted to disclose his lucky find. Just a few discreet questions he thought.

The following weekend Ed headed back, this time he'd brought his flatmate Paul as cover (no one could suspect Paul of anything except being under the influence) and he hoped they might pass as interested tourists.

As they drove down the narrow lanes and turned left towards the gates they noticed a large digger and a group of students. He pulled up outside and he and Paul walked towards them.

"Hello, could you tell me what's going on, are you the Circle Trust?"

One of the students, in jeans a woollen jumper with a bright plastic Mack over the top turned to answer.

"Hi, can I help, I'm Jenny from the University dig team"

Ed thought back to his map and was not pleased to here the word "dig" from somebody else's mouth.

"Oh we, my friend and I, had just come out to see the house and wondered what was going on?"

"I'm sorry the house is closed as far as I know, the Trustees have locked it up, something to do with an impending sale from the Council, its all very legal and complicated. That's why we're here, to have a dig around before anyone can get planning to build a housing estate or supermarket" Jenny laughed, "though who knows we might find the lost treasure too!" she added as a joke.

Ed went cold but quickly gathered himself and tried to say it as a joke with as little panic as possible "lost treasure?"

"Oh sorry, don't you know about Lord John Skuggborne of Skuggsby Hall?"

JS! Was this the JS on the cypher and beneath the crest on the vellum he had left with Professor Blickstone?

"No, I don't know, sorry have you got time to tell me?"

"Oh sorry its nothing really, just the last member of the family who owned this land, he was something of an Elizabethan philosopher, popular at Court for a while, he fell out of favour with Queen and not long after vanished along with his believed considerable fortune, but its just local gossip if you ask me. Sorry I've got to go we have to get the digger up the earth works to the circle, wish us luck we might even find a Neolithic burial"

"Good luck" said Ed half heartedly, he returned to the car with Paul, who had been chatting up one of the other diggers.

"Think I've got a date there mate" said Paul.

Ed determined to visit Professor Blickstone that day and see if he'd been able to decode the cypher.

Later that day at Professor Blickstone's house (academics of a certain age did not stay in College over the weekend) Ed arrived.

The professor welcomed him in "Come on in, sit down, I'm afraid I haven't had much luck with that document you left me."

"The cypher?"

"Yes an impossible thing, but no wonder given who wrote it" The Professor smiled in that way a person does when they've found something out they think you don't know.

"Who did write it?" Ed asked, hoping it might have been the last Tudor incumbent of Skuggsby Hall.

"Well" the Professor sat in his wing armchair near the open fire and placed his hands together, signalling this would be a lengthy discourse. "It was the distinctive Crest and Initials on the other piece that gave me the clue. I sent a picture, I hope you don't mind me sending a picture?"

Ed just hurriedly shook his his head "Not at all".

"I sent a picture to a colleague at the College of Arms in London. He knew immediately, its quite a well known Tudor crest you see, it belonged to Lord John Skuggsbourne."

"Oh, whose he?" Ed asked pretending, quite convincingly this time, to have never heard the name.

"Not much written about now, but quite famous, or should I say notorious in his day. I did a bit of digging around and found a mention of him, he apparently was quite the favourite in Elizabeth's court, well for a while and is rumoured to have devised ciphers for Walsingham, quite impossible ones also whilst publishing several Treatise on Ancient Languages.

"Vocabularum Antiquum Britannica" was one of his, but no complete copies appear to exist now, just an odd title page in the British Museum.

He seems to have secured his fortune by being given the Monopoly to produce gaming cards in 1578, though that was withdrawn in 1584, when he fell out of favour in Court and retreated back to live in Staffordshire. Here, I've found a picture of some.

Professor Blickstone got up and went over to his desk and pulled out a few sheets fresh from the printer.

"Here" he handed them to Ed. It was a beautifully illustrated Gaming card but did not have the suits we are familiar with today, Skuggsbourne's cards had suits in clubs (heavy wooden ones), Sickles, Circles and Suns.

"I think" said the Professor "that the design became popular in the Iberian Peninsula, you can still find similar sets in use today, though not identical. It's unlikely, if it is a complex Cypher, that I'll be able to decode it Ed, sorry, but the provenance it adds to the two pieces will certainly generate a lot of interest if you wanted to sell them?"

Ed could feel an offer coming from the Professor and usually that would be the main event, a good profit! But he had hoped for more explanation and insight to the relevance of the Map he had still not shown anyone.

"What happened to him?" Ed asked, you say he fell out favour in Court?

"Oh, some trouble with the Church, a pamphlet published in 1583 on the merits of Copernican Theory and how Pagan cultures had known that the Earth wasn't the centre of the Solar system. Quite controversial stuff at the time. No he went back to Staffordshire but shortly after was never seen or heard of again. I believe the family home passed to a distant relative but there was no fortune with it and it was quickly sold on."

"Well thanks anyway, its fascinating stuff" Ed lied.

"If you want I can keep trying and see if I can get anywhere"

"Yeah, okay" I'll leave you to it replied Ed and he drove off, it was now quite late, they'd been in conversation longer than he thought. He'd go home and get a good nights rest.

On entering the flat there was a thick cloud of dense sickly smoke in the flat and the stereo was pumping out deafening techno, he could hear laughing coming from the sitting room.

"Alright mate, any joy with your, what was it, Tudor Sudoku?"

Paul laughed. He was sat on the floor with the pretty young girl from the dig, "This is Hannah"

Hannah waved a half hearted hello, and Ed tried to strike up a conversation.

"So how's the dig going up at the Hall Hannah? Found anything?" He really hoped she'd say no.

"Yeah, it's going well, we found a few large quartz stone in the centre of the circle on the large Earth works, all very spooky!" She lent forward and waved her arms like a ghost and fell back laughing with Paul, it was clear that whatever they had both been smoking had taken full effect. Ed went straight to bed.

The next morning a quieter, more hung over Hannah greeted Ed in the kitchen. "Morning, where's Paul?"

"Still asleep, I'm just going to have a quick bit of Tea and Toast if that's ok and then just slip off?"

"Sure" said Ed, "The Tea bags are in the second cupboard, bottom shelf, I'll have one too if you're making one"

They sat at the table, more lucid than the previous night so Ed gave it another go.

"How's the dig going?"

"Oh fine" Hannah was in full possession of her faculties and glad to have something to talk about, rather that than an awkward silence. "We're carefully going around in cross sections, finding some large polished white and black quartz in odd positions inside the circle, but we haven't dated them, of course we keep coming up against all the robbed out holes which is a pain."

"Robbed out?" Ed enquired, slightly panicking, "Someone's been digging before you?"

"Oh no, not recently, it's all the treasure hunters and that stupid story" Ed remembered what Jenny had mentioned to him at the Hall when he'd gone back that day, but she'd been in too much of a rush to tell him.

"What story?" Hannah sipped her Tea, "Make us some toast and I'll tell you", Ed quickly obliged.

"The Lord of the Hall was supposed to have become obsessed with the stone circle, he wouldn't leave it and return to court, that and some heretical views (Ed recalled the Copernican Pamphlet the Professor mentioned as he was listening) meant he fell out of favour. Not long after it was believed he had died but there was no record in the Parish register of a burial. His Steward, an old Welshman called John Emrys, sold all his chattels the following month for a recorded £7000 in gold and silver coin, a fortune at the time but then disappeared. Anyone with half a brain will know he probably murdered his Master and ran off with the money, no mystery at all. However there were rumours, just gossip if you ask me, that Emrys buried his Master with his fortune in a Pagan ritual ground, which of course everyone took to be the Stone Circle and they've been digging it up ever since, and now so are we! Thanks for the toast."

Hannah left and for the first time Ed had an idea of what the map he had found might be, could it be the resting place of Lord John Skuggsborne and his fortune?

He went to his room and removed the map from the locked drawer in his desk where he had kept it. He traced the feint red line from the Hall up the hill to the circle and then along, down to the Coppice marked with a ring of trees and the black square. This time the lettering he couldn't make out before seemed readable, "Emrys Fidelem" was written below and above "Spec, Specu, possibly Speculum". This might be it.

That evening Paul would be out with Hannah, it was a party for one of the diggers birthdays in town and they were doing the curry mile, he'd been invited but declined. Now, he thought would be a perfect time to take a look, the site should be unoccupied and he'd take his metal detector along just in case.

He pulled up along the estate wall in the narrow lane. The walls were in a state of disrepair in parts and here it was low enough for him to step over, he'd got a torch, bag, detector and a small spade and pry bar (just in case). He made his way across the open fields towards the circle which he could just about make out in the moonlight, the house he saw was silhouetted dark and empty to the right and to the left the hill ran away down to the coppice, marked on his ordnance survey as what was left of the Ancient "Gattaker Wood". He stumbled forward, loosing the bag, "Bugger! he cried. Hannah had not been wrong when she said they had been digging. There were short trenches all around the Stone Circle, he picked himself up and proceeded more carefully as he went, this time with the torch held low to the ground as the moon kept clouding over and he needed to see where he was going.

The torch fluoresced slightly against a stone, one of the quartz stones in the ground, it was surprisingly bright in the darkness, then a little further on, another smaller and off set, Ed stopped and shone around the torch, he could make out eight or nine quartz stones all of differing sizes around a central larger stone in the very middle of the circle. You could have walked straight past them normally but they seemed to respond to the light in the pitch darkness of night. He pulled the Map out of his jacket pocket and proceeded down a rough path which seemed to correspond to where the faint red line had been drawn.

Moving throughout the wild meadow towards the small

Coppice, he didn't notice the two fallen, overgrown stones he stepped directly through as the Moon appeared from behind the clouds in the sky casting his shadow forward. He took nine long steps forward and thought this is where the black square marked on the map should be, he got out his detector and began to scan the woodland floor. He'd got a weak single and then hit something, hard. He put the detector down and felt into the soft wet undergrowth, pushing small roots, earth and rotting leaves to one side. He could feel something hard and smooth, tracing the edges of it with his fingers, he cleaned off the edges, it was square, perfectly so but with small notches running around the edge. He tried to lift it, it was bedded in, he took the pry bar from his bag and forced it under an edge, it was quite thin and he was worried he might crack it like a tile, but he levered it up and began to rub the surface clean. The stone was black, it looked for all the world like a huge piece of Obsidian and he could now see that the notches running all around the edge were the same as on the Crested vellum square he had left with Professor Blickstone. He peered into the centre of it, it was polished as fine as a mirror and as he did so the Moonlight cleared again, he saw his face reflected in it and then it was not his face. A terrible cry went up and the rookery of crows within the wood screeched and all flew up at once in the night sky.

It was three months later, Professor John Blickstone had grappled with the cypher Ed had left him to no avail. He'd compared them to known Walsingham decrypted codes of the period but he could only ever get a few words, Mirror, King's, Sphere, Heaven's Life which made no sense at all. He had not heard from Ed and thought it long overdue to return the parchments to their rightful owner. He had not answered any calls or emails so, as it was a quiet afternoon he would go to the flat and return them himself. Not a half hour later he had arrived at Ed's door.

He rang the bell. "Hello" said Paul to Professor Blickstone, "Can I help?"

"Oh hello, I just called around to return these to Ed, he left them with me a few months ago but I haven't got anywhere with them I'm afraid"

"Ed, oh Ed's not here anymore, haven't you heard? Come in"

Paul showed the Professor in and sat him down at the kitchen table, after removing a few uncleaned cereal bowls and ashtrays. "Yeah, Ed don't live here no more" "Nothings happened to him has it?" Professor Blickstone asked. "Well yes and no, nothing's happened in the way you mean, nothing dreadful like. He's won the lottery."

"Lottery?"

"Well as good as. It was about three months ago an old relative, from Wales, I didn't know he had any Welsh in him, an old relative died and left him a stack of money, millions they say. Changed him a bit though, became very self important, no time for me anymore, though he left me the flat when he moved which was kind of him"

"Moved? Where to?"

"Well besides his millions, this old Welsh relation had run a company or trust, I can't quite remember which" Paul began to roll and light and home made cigarette. "Yeah funny, they had just bought an old house from a council that got left to him too, it was a bit of wreck but he moved straight in, he's there now, doing the place up, it's costing a fortune"

"Oh, well what do you think I should I do about these papers of his?"

"My girlfriend will remember the address, she worked on a dig there a while back, funnily I met her when Ed took me up there one weekend. Hannah!"

Hannah came out of the bedroom, "Morning, oh hello"

"Hannah this the Professor, he's a mate of Ed's and wanted to get in touch to give these back"

Hannah walked to the kitchen table and looked at the two old parchments, "Oh, are you a professor of Archaeology?" she assumed. "No Medieval and Tudor studies" Blickstone replied "Why do you ask?"

"Well its not every day you seem someone carrying around a copy of an Ogham inscription" she pointed not to the elaborate page of cyphers but the perfect vellum square on which John Skuggsborne's crest had been drawn, "These here, the lines at angles around the edge, it's Ogham, or at least it looks like Ogham script, might be earlier"

"Do you know what it says?"

"No, not really, its hard to translate and there's still some discussion as to wether its a language or a Druidic cypher for one"

Professor Blickstone was slightly gobsmacked and

overwhelmed with curiosity but knew he must return the papers to Ed, maybe now, with his new found wealth he might let him keep them for all the research he'd undertaken?

"Do you have Ed's address, I'd like to take these back in person"

"Sure its Skuggsby Hall, Staffordshire, here I'll print you off a Google Map"

A day or two later Professor John Blickstone was driving along a small narrow road bordering an estate brick wall which was undergoing a great deal of expensive restoration. He turned left at a T-junction and proceeded through an impressive wrought iron gate, now highlighted in gilt, possibly by the ironworker Jean Tijou, up a gravel drive to a resplendent Tudor Manor, the timbers freshly blackened an the walls a vibrant limed white. To the side a lawn was being removed and box hedging planted to restore the original Knot garden. He knocked on the door and a small elderly man greeted him,

"Good morning sir, you must be Professor Blickstone, do follow me" he detected a faint Welsh accent.

"Who is it?" called a stern clear voice from the library.

"Professor Blickstone to see you Master Edward"

They walked through the main corridor, it was sumptuously decorated in hanging tapestry and rich dark carved Elizabethan Oak with polished brass and carved and painted armorials mounted above.

As they turned into the library, now heaving in ancient leather bound tombs, the Professor could not help but admire a superb gilt brass Orrery on the table beside him, signed and dated "JS 1584", though that of course had to be apocryphal, Orreries weren't made to that complexity until the later part of the eighteenth century? There were fine astrolabes and globes too, and a superb copy? of a reflecting telescope, a large one which looked early, impossibly so, not Tudor, it couldn't be. With all this to admire he'd almost forgotten the purpose of his visit.

"Hello, Professor Blickstone"

Ed stood in front of him, clearly, but his posture and bearing had changed, it was more confident and authoritarian, and his clothing was tailored and immaculate, Savile Row had also clearly benefited from his good fortune.

"Take a seat won't you, I hear you've had no luck with that cypher, never mind"

"Yes I'm afraid I could only decode a couple of words at best, but I did find out the other parchment..."

"Yes?" Ed interjected

"...the other parchment is more interesting than we thought, the random lines around the edge may be in an early Druidic script called Ogham"

"Not Ogham, I think" replied Ed with steely certainty, "It's a much earlier version of that particular alphabet, though it shares much the similar base route, much harder to decipher though, it could take one years, even with the ability to fully translate and decipher the inscription" he paused "but a worthwhile, very worthwhile endeavour nonetheless" Ed smiled a cold, hard smile and continued, though Skuggsborne's cypher is far less demanding.

The Professor looked taken aback and offended that his months of effort were being dismissed in an instance.

"Oh really, I suppose you can read it?!" he exclaimed.

"Indeed" replied Ed, "It's child's play"

He took up the parchment and only half paying attention to it began to clearly read:

"this seventh day of the first month 1584. my servant Emrys has today assisted me and cleared off all the soil within the circle. It can be seen from white and polished stones of different placement and dimension a map of the heavens, specific in every detail, nine around one. I have related the calculation to the Copernican ideals and shall now endeavour to construct a working model, though infinitely smaller than our Ancient forbears did, to predict the next alignment. Though the translation on the *Speculum Regale* for which our lands are named goes slow a pace"

"this twentieth day of the second month 1584. The model is complete and it calculates that it shall not be four hundred years hence until the next alignment, though the *Konungs Skuggsja* is nearly ready to give up its final secrets and the last few symbols upon the four edges become clear to me. At an appointed time and place, the mirror must be raised in moonlight to pass one soul to another, as the Pagan King's did to live once more, willingly and freely. I shall set Emrys and his forbears with half my fortune to instruct it so. He shall place me to rest beneath the blackstone until then"

"Fascinating isn't it Professor and not hard at all, but I should not wish to keep you from your valuable studies. Thank you for the safe return of MY papers, my steward will see you out. Emrys!"

The Hawthorn Cross

It was a crisp February Monday morning and Rob was fumbling through a bunch of keys one handed, struggling to open the gallery door. The other was occupied holding a large coffee from the cafe at the top the street which he called into as regular as clockwork before opening. As he rattled through to find the right key (why was it always the last one?) the coffee let out plumes of steam into the cold morning air through the small hole in the cover like a tiny steam train.

He'd got the right one at last and the door opened, pushing against a small mound of post which had accrued over the weekend, the foot of the door swept it away.

Placing the Coffee on his desk, which was straight before him but at the back of the shop, he returned to close the open door and collect the mail, he swung the leather satchel from his shoulder onto a waiting chair as usual, in one single well rehearsed daily ritual.

"Bill, Bill, Bill..." he proceeded to pile up the correspondence on the left hand side of his desk and he sat sipping the now slightly cooled coffee from its polystyrene holder, "Oh, Catalogue!"

The thick fat brown envelope he just opened had a catalogue from Gareth & Rawlings, a small estate agency down in the West Country for the "Sale of the contents of Deventree Rectory, near Glastonbury".

Years ago, twenty in fact, when Rob had first started dealing in Antiques, (well anything back then), a daily flurry of catalogues fell through the letter box, that was the norm. Nowadays though everything was streamlined and online, Auctioneers rarely sent you out printed catalogues, they just emailed a link or a reminder bleeped on your phone.

No one really held house sales either, unless they were "put up jobs" where an Auctioneer had found a near empty Stately property and filled it with old trade goods to sell, adding value, or so they hoped, by the association.

Any association added by coming from a Rectory in Somerset would be of little or no value and it really wasn't worthwhile for the Auctioneers to orchestrate one. It must, he thought, be one of those rare instances where an Estate Agents had got a property to sell with its contents still intact, holding the sale at the house being so much easier than shifting it lock, stock and barrel to a local Auction House.

"Might just be a worth look" he thought, though it was less a commercial decision, more driven by his own nostalgia for the days of his youth, driving around the country like a mad man, looking for anything worthwhile, hidden treasures, to sell.

Since those early days he had moved up in the world of Antiques and now specialised in "Kuntskammer", 17th and 18th century Works of Art, boxes, carvings, religious artefacts, mainly, but not exclusively, from Europe. His gallery (no one called them shops anymore) had been set up five years ago and was a great success. A small but perfectly formed shop in one of the quieter Kensington streets, the double fronted windows were faintly, tastefully painted in gold lettering "Robert Autrey Works of Art".

The display was all very low key, beautifully lit with floral arrangements and rows of dark wooden display cases to the left and right, with irregular shelving to offset the myriad of small copper gilt and enamel boxes, carved wooden figures, reliquaries, hardstones and ivories, mixed in with natural curios that filled the gallery. Rob's desk was opposite the door so he could immediately engage with any casual custom, peering up from behind the opened upright screen of his laptop.

It was now just after nine and the door opened. "Morning Mr Autrey" said an immaculately dressed young woman, though struggling with a series of folders under one arm and yet another Costa coffee cup in the other.

"Morning Kate" Rob replied without looking up from the screen, unaware one folder was heading for the floor and the coffee cup was precariously near to tipping over.

"I spoke to Dr Darscholt over the weekend, he's going to take those two South German boxwood figures. Can you generate an invoice now and email it to him, then get onto the shippers (the old firm of Wander and Lyle) and see of they can get them to him in Dresden by the end of the week, earlier if at all possible?"

"I'll get straight on it, anything else urgent?"

Rob looked down at the catalogue that had just arrived, "Yes after that book me a train to a place called Deventree, it's in Somerset near Glastonbury next Wednesday and try and find me some local accommodation overnight."

Just over a week had passed and Rob found himself enjoying a very pleasant train journey down to the West Country. He was enjoying it all the more as the two seventeenth century carved boxwood figures, Allegories from a set of the four seasons, Spring and Autumn, had been delivered to a Dr Darscholt in Dresden and found a new home. The bank transfer payment for, even by his standards, a good price, had only just cleared that morning into his account and here he was heading down to an old fashioned house sale with money to burn.

He thought it advisable to go through the sale catalogue as he journeyed down, even though he'd scanned through it quickly a couple of times already. He took the catalogue out, placed it neatly on the table before him and withdrew a fine Parker pen from the inside pocket of his jacket. As he opened the catalogue he began to meticulously run down each lot number in turn, pausing only to faintly circle any lot which might be of particular interest.

"Lot 48, Georgian bracket clock, ebonised and gilt A/F"

That sounded promising, he circled it. All the descriptions were happily brief and without too much detail that might alert the casual viewer to a hidden gem, though "A/F" (as found) was appearing in the catalogue more than he had hoped.

He ran through lots of porcelain, paintings, some silver, then the furniture. "Lot 211 Georgian close stool" sounded worth a look. He was hoping it would be a rich dark Cuban mahogany trap top commode with all its original brass work made around 1770 and not a hideous orange job from the reign of George IV, or even Victorian. After all "Georgian" was a pretty hit and miss term in most catalogues these days. After that it was pretty much boxes of household effects, then garden and domestic fittings.

It briefly occurred to him he might have built this sale up a little in his mind and it could be a colossal waste of time, well he'd know for sure tomorrow.

He got into Glastonbury in the afternoon and took a cab to the nearest local pub by "Deventree Rectory" which appeared to almost be in the middle of nowhere, oddly there did not appear to be a nearby Church?

Arriving at the "Old Bush" he tried not to laugh, he went to check in and get a meal, fully expecting straw hat chewing locals and thick clotted cream accents, he was quite surprised how tasteful and modern it all was inside.

"Good afternoon, can I help" came a distinctly home counties voice over the bar. The barman was, he found from a brief chat whilst checking in was also the proprietor James (Jim to the locals) Sellek.

"As in Magnum P.I?" Rob joked but could immediately see he was only about the thousandth person to do so, probably that year.

"No, sadly we all lack a vital "c" and the obligatory bushy moustache." His host had been kind enough to take it in good humour and given him the let out. He thought it best to order a large whisky and retire to a vacant corner of the bar next to what would soon be a roaring fire.

"Have you eaten, we'll be serving dinner in about half an hour?"

"No, no I haven't and I didn't get anything on the train down, a good home cooked meal would definitely hit the spot."

"Sit down, I'll bring a menu over with your whisky in a minute."

The whole air of the bar was very civilised, natural wood. Tasteful, but not stuffy views of the local area mounted up alongside old newspaper articles from the "Glastonbury Chronicle" and old photographs, probably Victorian, blown up and printed alongside, this was definitely the "Waitrose" of country hostelries.

Rob sat down, put his bag by his side and placed the catalogue unopened on the table next to his phone as he checked for messages, the reception on the train down had been awful.

"Here's your Whisky (it came in suitably heavy and well cut glass) and the menu, the steak and ale pie with roasted winter veg is pretty spot on"

"Thanks, I'll have that then when the kitchen's ready" Rob had lived and dined out in London long enough not to refuse a simple steak pie when it was offered.

"Oh" said Jim noticing and pointing to the closed catalogue on the table, "Is that what you're here for, the sale at the Old Gaol?"

"Gaol? I thought it was a Rectory, at least that's what it says in the catalogue." Rob replied.

"Yes, it was a Rectory for a long time, up until quite recently, but before that, parts of it were the Old Gaol, it's what any of the local families around here would still call it if you were to ask."

"Is it far from here? The map in the catalogue's a bit rudimentary and they don't give a postcode so it's a bugger trying to Google Map it"

Jim pointed towards a window opposite looking out onto some fields, "a brisk 10-15 minute walk if you're up for it and you're there. Besides the walk is almost straight, if you went by car you'd have to go round half of the village and it would take as long"

"Right, I'll walk there in the morning, could you write me the directions down when you've got a minute"

"Sure, no problem" replied Jim.

The evening passed easily, the fire was warm, the whisky excellent and the Steak pie had a suet crust like gold and was in every respect, from tender meat to thick rich gravy, delicious. If there was nothing at the sale tomorrow Rob determined that "The Old Bush" would be a regular call anytime he was in this neck of the woods. He went to his room and slept soundly and half drunk.

The next morning the insistent shrill alarm he'd set on his phone woke him. He got dressed and set off early to get to the Rectory to view, the sale would commence at 11.00 am and he thought he needed at least two full hours to view everything he had marked down and then do some general quick browsing of the rest.

He'd got his phone which he'd remember to charge the night before, thank God! Wallet, catalogue and the simple directions Jim had written down.

"Go right up the lane to Frenchman's corner, the turn left down the track to the gated field, walk straight across and look to your left, then underlined YOU CAN'T MISS IT!

It was as crisp and cold a morning as he'd known, very quiet in the village which was all set back custodial or tied thatch with the odd small Georgian brick house thrown in for good measure. The tree's were still leafless and a hoar frost covered the branches of the hedgerow bushes, he continued up the road until he came to a cross roads with a large hewn stone plinth and a horse trough with weathered oak posts for tying the animals beside it. He'd seen these before in villages, they would be where the Stocks would be placed, or in more serious cases a make-shift wooden gibbet erected. This was the place known locally as Frenchman's corner.

He duly turned left as instructed and crossed the field. He then realised why Jim in the bar had been insistent he would not miss it. Rather than a small timber framed building reminiscent of any number of Miss Marple Vicarages or Rectories there stood a large Gothic octagonal stone tower, four storeys high with a crenellated turret. He immediately quickened his step to take a closer look.

Indeed, when he approached and could see it clearly, it was a very pleasing tower, not early Gothic, the lancet windows on each subsequent floor were too wide with swollen ogee arches and carved trefoil decoration for that, maybe circa 1500? What couldn't be mistaken was a chocolate box Victorian timber framed addition at the base, more Cadbury's than Norman-Shaw. He took his phone to get a couple of pictures, firstly because it really was an unusual piece of West Country architecture, but secondly it would really help to sell anything he might buy if he had a picture of the property that it had come from to accompany it.

As he approached up the winding graveled path he got to a large Oak hobnailed door with a massive wrought iron ring handle, somewhat over engineered for a Rectory, but perfect one might suspect for a Gaol. At the base of the tower was thick cut down tree stump at the right hand side as you went in, very much in the way, almost blocking the path to the door, odd, Rob wondered, that no one had thought to remove it.

Inside, even though he'd arrived quite early, he was saddened to see several familiar faces, many were local dealers he'd known for years who would only ever bid so much on anything, so weren't competition for a really good lot, but there were at least two London faces he was sincerely hoping not to see, one approached him.

"Hello, Rob, why have you come all the way down here?" enquired Peter, a dealer so long in the London trade that there was not a person he did not know.

"It's my sister's wedding this weekend" he quickly lied, "she only lives a couple of miles away so I thought I'd come down a couple of days early and do this too" (he did not even have a sister).

"Well good luck, if there's anything you really fancy come and have a chat in a bit" Which was the familiar code, from Peter, to say we'll work out how much you've got to pay me not to bid on anything you really want. Rob's spur of the moment wedding ploy had failed to impress, especially as it was the middle of February.

He began to look around, it was a really traditional sale. The auctioneers hadn't much moved anything, it was all like a favourite Great Aunt's house, clutter untouched for fifty years. He'd managed to find Lot 48, the bracket clock (though he would more correctly call it a table clock if selling). It was quite nice, a three pad case in ebony with gilt brass edges and carrying handles signed "John Thomas of Crewkerne" and looked about 1750, the engraved foliate backplate was good enough and it had finely turned baluster pillars, but it didn't run and the bell (or bells) and pendulum were missing. He really didn't fancy footing an expensive restoration bill for a provincial example. The Georgian commode had been an unspeakable horror, though there was an impressive early 18th century walnut chest on chest, with canted and stop fluted corners and lovely original bail handles, but it too, was worse for wear, badly faded and it would take up so much room back in the Gallery for very little profit, still it might have to be that than come away empty handed.

By now Rob had worked his way up to the very top floor of the tower. The final floor was totally bare in furnishings, no carpet, no wall coverings, just a simple stone octagon with a small fireplace and a lancet window, above there was a small hatch which he thought might lead to the crenellated roof, if a ladder had been there he would have been tempted to go up.

Here were ten or so boxes of "Household Items", it was still a hour until the auction started so he began to look through. A couple of boxes of prayer books, to be expected at any worthwhile Rectory sale, some Victorian brass candlesticks, gothic only in style, a box a vestments. This, he thought must be where they stowed all the God kit. The next box appeared to be full of small bronze, copper and silver souvenir medallions, but all religious, all with saints on, in fact, as he looked closely all depicting the Archangel Michael in one form or another, also there was a small Victorian cloth bound publication "Deventree, its History and Customs by the Rev J.P.Sellek" and, at the very bottom he pulled out a wooden cross.

To call it a wooden cross was to do it a disservice, it was about 6 inches long and superbly and finely carved with blossoms across the top and bottom sides and a intricate networks of thorns and branches all around the sides. It looked to be 18th century carving at the very least and by an extremely skilled hand.

The top of the cross had a suspension ring carved into it as an integral piece such as you might find on Welsh love spoons, but rather than simple rings it was a foliate trefoil and below that was a fine small five knuckle hinge, "it must open!" thought Rob. Frustratingly the small hook catch at the base of the cross had been removed and a brass nail hammered in to keep it closed, also three bundles of blackened wire had been twisted around the ends of the cross very tightly indeed so there was no chance of opening it now. Rob thrust if back, deep, into the bottom of the box, covered it over with the medallions and made a note of the lot number.

The sale started at a brisk pace, but it could not be brisk enough for Rob, he imagined what could be inside the cross, perhaps a carved scene or the Crucifixion, or perhaps a reliquary? Whatever it was he felt that Dr Darscholt in Dresden might want to give it a new home as he had just done Spring and Autumn. Rob was determined.

Peter bought the Crewkerne table clock and Rob made a show of staying out of it, bidding very lowly once and then dropping out. This, he hoped, would placate Peter and indeed, before the last household lots were up for sale, Peter had already paid and left with the clock, Rob hoped the field would be clear.

"Lot 369, household items, medals, a book various" announced the Auctioneer, "Do I see twenty, ten pounds?" Rob lifted his catalogue up about half an inch to indicate an bid, and without any further interest the hammer fell. Rob tried not to turn a cartwheel, rather gathered himself, paid and then hurriedly left.

Even carrying the box it was not long before he was back in his room at "The Old Bush" and tipping out the contents on the table before him.

The medals were not great, most nineteenth or twentieth century, he wouldn't sell them in the Gallery but they could all be put online and make at least two or three hundred which covered most of his costs thus far. The book, only a small vanity publication of the sort which abounded by industrious clergy in the early nineteenth century could be put aside for a bedtime read (better than a sleeping tablet) and then, there was the cross.

Rob examined it carefully, he had thought in the dim light of the fourth floor of the tower it should be lime or boxwood, but he could see now it was clearly neither, the outer parts of the cross were lighter, could it be Yew he thought? Rare if it was. The carving was very fine and delicate, it reminded him of something he'd seen at the V&A some years ago, German, French? He'd have to check, but the quality of it was undeniable. He was tempted to leave the removal of the brass nail and the wire to his restorer, but curiosity just got the better of him. He took out the nail scissors from his travelling bag and snipped the fine wires, he then took the point and eased the nail out from behind, until he could grab it and pull, it freed itself easily. He checked a damaged hinge wasn't the reason it was nailed and bound shut in the first place, it moved easily and was intact, he then carefully opened it.

Much to his surprise the interior did not have a Saint's bone, or a depiction of Christ on the cross, instead he was looking at a minute, fine carving of the Tower he had just been in! At the foot was a bush in bloom with what appeared to be thick thorns protruding through. Every detail was there, the bound oak iron door with it's ring handle and the ogee topped lancet windows on each successive floor topped with the crenellated turret.

He noticed the inside of the cover was carved with a short inscription in Latin "IVSTITA ENIM DEI EST" and the initials "L.F" and a date "1692". Rob could hardly contain his excitement, but he now hoped he could attribute the carving to a specific artist, thereby dramatically enhancing its value.

He closed the cross and carefully wrapped it in his pocket, the other pieces from the lot he just stuffed into his travelling bag. He then went down to the bar until it was time to catch the train for London that evening.

Once back in Gallery he called Dot. He'd known Dot (Dr Dorothy Pineward) for many years and had even lent her specific pieces when she wanted to hold an exhibition of later European carving at the V&A (where she was a deputy keeper) early last year.

"Dot, I wondered if I could come up tomorrow and have a refresher on seventeenth century carving, look at a few examples from the stores? No, no specific reason, just nothing on and wondered if you were free?"

He had, of course, a very specific reason, finding an attribution for his cross, but the very best Dealers are wary of showing their cards early on, the very best Dealers often won't even let you know that they are playing. Besides if it was that important even the Museum might be interested and he didn't want them to know he'd just bought in a box lot for a tenner.

The next morning he arrived by taxi at the tradesman's entrance of the V& A, and after a bag search and phone call "upstairs" was allowed to wend his way up and down through dark corridors and narrow stairways, he came to the office door and knocked loudly.

"Dot, lovely to see you" all the usual pleasantries were exchanged, he'd even brought a gift, nothing much, a lovely French devotional pendant of the Archangel Michael (one of the cheaper copper ones that had come in the lot)!

Dr Pineward had gotten out a small selection of carvings, all wood and all seventeenth century as Rob had requested. There were some fine lime and box German carvings together with a crude Iberian example, the pieces which immediately took Rob's eye were a small selection of boxes, he picked one up and began examining it.

"Ah yes Cesar Bagard" uttered Dot, "very fine work but probably nothing to do with him"

Rob narrowed his eyes and threw her a questioning glance which signalled for her to tell him more.

"They were all carved in Nancy in the Duchy of Lorraine out of Bois-de-Saint Lucie (a type of Cherry wood). All highly skilled craftsmen and Bagard was the most famous, so everything gets attributed to him, but there were several families who carried out the carving. Dom Culmet in his "Bibliotheque Lorraine" mentions that the Foulon family were very well known and made pieces for the Dauphin. When Nicholas Foulon died in 1698 they made an inventory of his workshop which included boxes, powder boxes, brushes, tobacco rasps, crucifixes...

"Crucifixes?" interrupted Rob.

"Yes, but.." Dot's eyes scanned the table "I don't think the Museum has got one of their's though we do have this beauty"

She picked up an oval carved portrait of an astonishingly beautiful young woman in late seventeenth century dress. It was in profile and very reminiscent of the fine work of the Ivories of David Le Marchand, but all in a close grained wood, it was carved on the back EML and dated 1691, strikingly it was bordered with a frame of intricately carved blossoms.

"This is my favourite and may well have been carved by a French artisan working in this country. A colleague confirmed the style of dress to be English though the style is definitely reminiscent of the very best work from Nancy"

"She's, well it's beautiful" commented Rob as he examined it, the carved floral border almost entirely matched the blossom on the top and bottom of his cross.

"What do you think the Wood is?" asked Dot.

Academics always like to tease Dealers at least once every visit and ask them questions they know they'll get wrong. It had the same difference in colour as the cross too, less pronounced but there was a definite lighter edge to the border.

"Is it Yew?" Rob quite sensibly guessed.

Dot beamed, "No, you'll never guess, in fact we had so much discussion about ourselves that we had a chap at Kew take a look, its no less than Hawthorn"

"Hawthorn? That's an odd choice isn't it?"

"Yes but even odder its not an everyday specie of Hawthorn, it's 'Crataegus monogyna biflora' commonly known as Glastonbury Hawthorn"

Rob looked blank.

"You know the one which flowers twice a year, fabled to have been brought to England by Joseph of Arimathea along with the Holy Grail. Oh you must know the Roundheads cut one down on Glastonbury Tor during the Civil War and all the locals got very upset."

Rob didn't know the story but the connections were beginning to fire off in his brain, surely the wood was the same and even if he couldn't put a name to the carver, the rarity of it must mean his cross was worth a small fortune. He couldn't keep it to himself any longer.

"Look Dot, I brought this along to show you, it's why I really asked for a refresher on the subject. I think it might be by the same hand"

He pulled the cross, carefully wrapped, out of his inside pocket and handed it to her. "It's not perfect, there's some discolouration caused by old metal wire, but the quality is superb, just look inside, it opens up."

Dot admired the beauty of the exterior of the cross and opened it, "Fascinating, a tower, do you know who these figures are yet?"

Figures? there were no figures, just the tower and the bush, Rob went to look.

Sure enough the tower was there but the bush had gone, just the vestige of an awkward cut stump remained. The door previously shut was opened and a tall clerical figure could be seen beside a young woman with her head in her hands weeping and a man, chained and in pain on the floor, there also appeared to be thorns (?) coming out of the first lancet window.

"Do you mind if I sit down?" Rob collapsed into the chair beside him "I, I couldn't have a hot sweet cup of tea could I?" He was suffering genuine shock at what he had just seen.

After a moment he told Dot about the cross and how it had NOT been that carving when he had opened it earlier, neither could arrive at anything approaching a reasonable explanation. Once Rob had recovered a little he left Dot, taking the cross with him but wrapping it up far tighter in his pocket than before.

That night he simply couldn't sleep wondering about the cross. He looked around for something to read and his hand alighted in his bag on "Deventree, its History and Customs by the Rev

J.P.Sellek" if this couldn't put him to sleep nothing would, he began to read a Chapter titled "Frenchman's corner"

"... it was sometime in the spring of 1691 that a French carver and gilder arrived in Deventree having passed up through Cornwall and The Channel Isles in fleeing the persecution of late under the French Regime and its Revocation of the Nantes Treatise. Mr Louis Foollon (sic) late of the region of Nancy came to settle and undertake to establish a business in all manner of wooden luxuries. He was at first welcomed into the area and completed many fine commissions for the local gentry, with carved furnishings supplied both to Montacute and Brympton D'Evercy. He is known to have befriended the Rector of Deventree and executed a fine carved roundel of his betrothed Elizabeth Mary Luscombe which was much admired around the Parish.

Later that year, despite success in his endeavours that Foollon was accused of felling the Holy or Old Bush which grew in the grounds of the Old Gaol with the Rector serving as witness. Foollon attested that the Rector had instructed him to fell it as a good substitute for his craft, being the better of the cherry wood of his native land. Some days later the Rector's betrothed, Elizabeth Luscombe was found, cruelly murdered with a cudgel said to be fashioned from the wood of the felled bush.

Foollon was held for several weeks in the top room of the Old Gaol tower and was then taken to the Taunton assizes, in a "poor and frail condition" only to be found guilty of the murder. He was hanged at specific request and urging of the Rector, a figure of some wealth and standing, at the old crossroads in Deventree where the stocks had been erected. His last words were to curse the Rector and to say that "Justice is for God". It was from that time on known as Frenchman's corner.

Shortly after, it is thought from grief caused by the loss of his beloved, that the Rector threw himself from the top of the tower of the Old Gaol, though foxes or wild beasts must have found him where he lain, due to much tearing and disfigurement of the flesh"

Rob went cold, were they the three figures on the cross? He had to look. He got up and went back downstairs turning on the lights as he went, taking the cross from out of the locked drawer he'd kept in. He tentatively opened it once more.

The figures had gone and now he all he could see was a Clergyman (surely the Rector) standing on top of the Tower and the thorns, the thorns that appeared to pierce the lower windows were now at the top, more prominent that before, almost claw like.

He had a thought, a terrible one and closed the cross tight, then immediately opened it once more. Sure enough, the carved scene had changed again, now the Rector was at the edge of the tower and he could see that thorns, were in fact talons, sharp claws on the hands of some hideous contorted creature, going towards the figure on the edge of the parapet. He closed it tight shut once more and dared not open it again, he got some thick chord out of the drawer and tied it tight shut.

The next morning Professor Dorothy Pineward came to work to find a parcel addressed to her, from Rob. It was a donation to the Museum Collection, a fine French carved devotional cross dated 1692 and signed by Jean Louis Foulon, a native of Nancy. Alongside it was a short note and a copy of "Deventree, its History and Customs by the Rev J.P.Sellek", she flicked through the pages to read a chapter which had been marked by the addition of a small clean slip of paper, it was titled "The Holy Bush"

"...it was believed to be planted and cut from the very one which Joseph brought to the Tor in the certain belief it would contain an ancient Pagan spirit and bind its malice with its roots. The belief in the story was indeed very strong as local folklore issued a grave warning that the sharp thorns were the talons of that beast trying to get out and that a terrible fate, of being torn asunder would befall any who felled this sacred tree..."

The Mourning Ring

"Where do you want to go for a holiday this year?" called Rachel from the kitchen, as the combined whistle from the boiling kettle and the low muttering of voices from the Today programme on Radio Four combined to drown out much of it.

"I'm in the shower, I can't hear, I'm in the shower!" came a loudly shouted reply. John stepped out of the cubicle, almost tripping over the sink as he did so, theirs was not a large flat. He dried himself off and threw on his clothes, their bedroom was small and there wasn't room for a proper wardrobe, everything was either crammed into the drawers of a small chest or just hanging. He walked through into the kitchen.

"What did you say?" Rachel had her back to him she was buttering toast and just about to take two eggs from a boiling pan of water,

"I said where do you want to go on holiday this year?"

"You know we can't babe, we're only half way to a deposit and if we have to spend another year in this pokey bloody flat..." Rachel knew John was about to list any number of sensible reasons why their current cramped accommodation was getting a bit too much, it was fine when they were students together, but not anymore, she interrupted in a soothing and slightly apologetic tone as she turned and placed the eggs and buttered toast on the table.

"I know, I was just hoping for a break."

John felt bad, he knew he was cracking the whip but they had to get a deposit together and despite scrimping and saving for the last two years they were at least four or five thousand pounds short, but he knew with their combined holidays coming up that they needed a break.

"Look, why don't we go up North and do a few churches, a lot of them do 'Glamping' now actually IN the church, it doesn't cost much?"

As students John and Rachel had bonded over their mutual love of old and historic buildings, often taking day trips out around the University of Nottingham where they had met. John had studied to become an Architect (though now he sadly worked in the Council's planning office) so his interest was clear. Rachel studied fine art and had a real love of all the aspects of design and decoration, she loved nothing more than finding a beautiful carved gravestone or tomb, indeed posts of those images she'd taken had started off the large following for her Instagram account which was now her main source of income.

The idea of getting back to the earliest days of their relationship immediately appealed and Rachel thought

"why not, yes lets do it, we could go around Durham and at least then we'd be sure of a treat with the Cathedral"

"Okay, let's do it, we'll have a proper look when I get back this evening, why don't you do Pevsner this afternoon and we can work out a route tonight"

John rushed out of the door clutching a half finished toasted egg sandwich and his jacket. Rachel cleared the kitchen table and then got on with her day job, which had only begun as a hobby at Uni.

She set the background up and put the camera on its secure mount, then she went into the living room and got out the small jewellery box her Mum had left her.

Rachel's Mother had been a part time Antiques Dealer, jewellery mainly and Rachel used to go around all the fairs with her on a Sunday, sports centres, villages halls, hotels, anywhere there was enough parking and a good large room for the rows of trestle tables and the Gordian tangle of extension cables for cabinet lights.

Rachel remembered sitting next to her Mum as a bustle of people would all come wanting to see a ring or a brooch or a bangle, she would help out and open the cases handing pieces back and forth, taking money and putting it the small locked metal tin they kept beneath the table cloth, or handing bags and tissue paper to her Mum to wrap things up.

It had been something that had stayed with her, so even at Uni she'd kept on doing the local fairs to top her meagre student loan. When social media came along she wasn't slow to take it up. At first she just posted all the images from the trips she'd taken with John, architectural details, tombstones, carved pews and memorial plaques, but soon, at John's suggestion, she started adding in some pieces of jewellery, little Victorian posy rings, the odd mourning brooch, but it all seemed to gel with the people who were following her. Soon she stopped paying to do the Sunday table top fairs altogether and focused on finding nice antique pieces to put online, they sold, she found, surprisingly quickly if the price was fair and now she had a following of over 8,000, it had become her day job without Rachel even noticing.

The hardest part now was finding the pieces to sell as over the years more and more people had started selling Antique Jewellery on Instagram, though she'd met a lot of like minded people and made a lot of friends through it too. She couldn't just go around the local fairs and markets as she once did, many of them had gone (with so many people now selling online)! She did go to small auctions but also found Carboots, weekly markets her best bet for a something at a reasonable price.

She got on with photographing a few new rings, a Victorian 15ct gold band inset with small turquoise forming a flower and a plain 9ct Edwardian gentleman's signet ring hallmarked for Chester 1905, both had sold by the end of the day, the signet to a private buyer in America and the flower ring to a budding trader who was up in Barnard Castle called Heather. They chatted a bit online and Rachel felt she knew her, she was a bit younger and was where she had been about four or five years ago, just starting out. She messaged her, that if she liked, Rachel could bring the ring up to her in a couple of weeks as she was going to be in the area on holiday and that it would be lovely to finally meet up. Heather agreed and said she was looking forward to it.

A couple of weeks had passed and John was driving the little blue polo up the M1 with a deal of determination as Rachel held her phone trying to keep a signal strong enough to get directions, "the Junction after this and we should see a sign posted for the M18"

"Are you sure that's the best way?"

"Yes John, for the thousandth time its M1, M18 then A1..."

John turned the radio up a bit louder and muttered "Alright" under his breath as the Cranberries linger drowned out the conversation and they headed North.

It was evening by the time they arrived in Barnards Castle, there had been a small detour when the phone signal dropped out completely and John had determined to go along the A66 and not the A67 nearly ending up in Carlisle, had it not been for Rachel's timely intervention when the connection to Google Maps was temporarily restored on her phone.

They'd booked into a Hotel for the evening, the trips one small luxury. Rachel had arranged to meet Heather the next morning and then they would take a leisurely drive up to Durham and then spend the first night "Glamping" in the church of St.John's Escomb, a pretty Anglo Saxon edifice.

The evening was spent in the local discussing the trip, any animosity over directions was out the window and the beer was good and cheap enough. They retired to bed that evening tired by their journey but happily they did not sleep much.

The next morning John had a terrible hangover and was still half asleep at 9.00 am, Rachel had got up and dressed.

"Get up you lazy bugger, its nearly nine. Look I'm going to be late meeting Heather if I wait for you, I said I'd be there for coffee at half past, get up if you can and walk down and join us but I'm not being late just because you got pissed last night" She playfully kicked his foot which was protruding out of the crumpled duvet, he just grunted what seemed like an "ok" but turned back and buried his head in the pillow.

It was a bright warm day and Rachel walked down from the hotel which was in the centre of town to a small cafe, Heather had said it was her Gran's and a perfect place to meet up.

Rachel got to "Thompson's Teas" less a traditional greasy spoon than a tea room. There were dark wooden round tables all with chequered red and white table cloths, a small vase of fresh flowers in the centre of each and traditional cut glass condiment frames (no tubs of plastic sachets), it was really charming.

"Hi, Rachel?" came a delicate voice from the table in the far corner,

"Yes, hello! Lovely to meet you Heather after all the chat online"

Rachel sat down, Heather must have been at least six or seven years younger than her, maybe nineteen perhaps twenty, twenty one at a push and had a very excitable and eager nature, though she appeared to be very nice.

"Oh. here's the ring you bought from me, hand delivered as promised"

"It's lovely, thank you" I've bought some of my other rings I thought you might like to see. I don't have a lot of the lovely things which you sell, but I do find the odd gem around in the local shops that other people seem to miss.

Heather placed a small Victorian red leather travelling jewel case on the table, only about five inches square with a silvered buckle clasp to the top, she unclipped it. The cover opened in two parts to reveal a velvet lined interior, two open compartments separated by a central holder for rings. On one side there were two or three small Georgian mourning brooches in unmarked gold, mounted with hairwork panels under glass with the name of the deceased and the date of death on the reverse, on the other side were a couple of art nouveau pendants inset with Pearls and Peridots, all again in unmarked low carat settings, but beautifully done, then there were the rings, a row of four posy and gypsy set Victorian examples to which Heather added the turquoise flower example she'd just bought from Rachel.

"Really nice" Rachel said in genuine admiration, "You've got a good eye, if you keep on like this you're going to do well" she wanted to encourage Heather who she could see was a bit a shy though didn't want to patronise her either.

"Thanks, it means a lot from you, you keep looking and if there's anything you like maybe you can buy something from me! I'll just get us a cup of tea, unless you prefer coffee?"

"No tea's fine, milk and one please"

It was as Heather got up to get the tea that Rachel first noticed the ring on her finger. Jewellery Dealers have an unfortunate and uncontrollable habit of noticing everyone's jewellery, rings, necklaces, bangles and will often be caught out by staring uncontrollably. Rachel couldn't help herself,

"What's that?" she said pointing to the ring.

"Oh that's, that's a ring my Gran gave me, its a family one"

"Could I have have a look?" Heather seemed hesitant, but Rachel persisted "If you don't mind?"

"Sure, here" Heather twisted the ring back and forth from her finger and placed it on the table's chequered cloth in front of Rachel and added "I'll just get those Teas"

Rachel picked it up. It was a thick broad yellow band, buttery in colour which must mean a high carat gold, running around the upper outside edges were thin bands of white and blue enamel flush with the surface, (she'd seen the white before, usually indicating it was for a child or maiden, but not the blue) and then a large unusual cross picked out in the same colour enamels with a small central stone, probably a simple rose cut diamond chip. Around the outer surface it had a band of gold lettering against a black ground "Nevilles Cross 1346, Restored Aug 1785", the inside was plain except for a maker's mark "ST" in script in a little rectangle which looked to be overstruck, a king's head and a lion, Rachel quickly and discreetly took a photo of it with her phone, then placed the ring back down on the table.

Heather returned with the tea in proper cups and saucers.

"This is simply lovely, a family ring you say?"

"Yes my Gran gave it to me, it was her Gran's before that and so on."

"Do you know what the inscription on it means?" asked Rachel.

"I know it commemorates the famous battle round here, Neville's cross, when the Scot's were turned back, we did that at school but I don't know what the other date means, or the marks on the inside."

Rachel was intrigued by it, it was in the style of a Georgian mourning ring but oddly unnamed and the coloured enamels were very unusual too. She had spotted something similar but nowhere near as elaborate some months ago in one of Fellows sales (a specialist firm of jewellery auctioneers in Birmingham) and tried to buy it, but it had made several thousand and this ring she thought was far more interesting. She also thought of the four or five thousand pounds she and John desperately needed if they were ever going to have enough of a mortgage deposit to move.

"Have you..." Rachel paused slightly with a twinge of guilt but continued "...ever thought about selling it?"

Heather looked not so much surprised but worried,

"It's a family piece and whilst I prefer the Victorian pieces my Gran made me swear NEVER to sell it before she gave it me."

"Oh, it's just its quite a valuable ring, I didn't know if you knew?" Rachel desperately tried to coax and tempt her.

"How much do you think it's worth?" though Heather looked almost as guilty as Rachel had felt for asking

"Oh, I think it might be worth as much as four or five hundred" and quickly added "I have a collector who loves this sort of thing, I'd probably be able to pay you the five."

Heather was young and had, despite it being a gift never really liked the ring without knowing why. Five hundred pounds would buy a lot of Victorian jewellery so, after a little more persuasion by Rachel she agreed to sell it.

Rachel bid her goodbye and said they must keep in touch, tightly clutching the ring in her coat pocket. She apologised for not having the cash on her and was grateful Heather had taken a cheque and agreed not to cash until Rachel was back from her holidays early next week and could get to the bank.

A noise then came from the back of the shop, Heather's Grandmother had come to open up for the lunchtime trade (by then it was almost eleven), "Did you have a nice time with your new friend?" She enquired.

"Yes I got this new ring, it's Victorian with a turquoise daisy" Heather had put it on and showed it to her Grandmother.

"Lovely darling, but where's YOUR ring?" The eagle eyed old woman asked.

"Er, erm, well Rachel liked it so much and offered such a good price and you know I've never really."

The old woman looked panicked and grabbed Heather by both her arms, leaning in close to her face

"Tell me you haven't sold it, you swore you'd never sell it!" by now her panic had turned to fear and tears were forming in her eyes.

Heather, distressed pulled out the cheque, trembling and showed it to her "she, she gave me this, but I'm not to cash it until next week, I'm sure it will be fine Gran"

The old woman snatched the cheque from her Granddaughters hand and without hesitation thrust it directly into one of the lit gas hobs on the cooker behind her, sighing "Thank God" as it burned.

"Gran!" shouted Heather "What are you doing?"

The old woman, now no longer fearful, just angry sternly took her Granddaughter's eye with hers in a fixed earnest gaze and said "saving your life my girl, you must NEVER profit from it, never profit from it" she muttered on. They never spoke of it again.

Rachel and John had a great time in Durham Cathedral when they'd got there, lots of images of Gothic arches and the obligatory shot with the 12th century Sanctuary Knocker (though this was now a replica with the original kept safe in the Cathedral Treasury). John was unable to resist making the standard poor joke about it being a pity that they didn't have a pair, which did not go down at all well. After they had taken a picture of every arch and window, of every carved pew and inscribed stone and were both thoroughly exhausted they left the Cathedral. He had offered to pay for coffee and cake in the restaurant opposite. It was a sunny and warm day, so they sat outside and as they enjoyed the homemade walnut cake, Rachel, armed with the Wifi password, took a moment to update her Instagram account with some of the images they had just taken. Whilst doing this she thought she would also message a picture of the marks on the ring she had just bought from Heather to an Antiques dealer she'd met on Instagram who might be able to tell her what they were. "Message Bill" she tapped on her display:

"Bill, Hi, hope alls well and you don't mind me sending you a pic of some odd marks on a ring I've just bought, any info much appreciated if you can, x R"

She sent if off and then the picture of the marks.

A few minutes later, whilst they were still sat at the table finishing the very last piece of cake, her phone buzzed and a reply to her message came up:

"Rachel, hi. Yes I do know the mark, its for a Newcastle Goldsmith called Samuel Thompson (II) but he worked in Durham. The other marks are the duty mark and gold standard, the duty mark came in in 1784 and Thompson died sometime in 1785 so you can date it quite precisely (she had not mentioned the inscription or dates on the ring to Bill at this point) rare thing. If it is for sale let me know. All the best Bill"

Rachel took this is a very good sign, it was a locally made ring and she knew the maker now, plus Bill had wanted to buy it, Bill had only ever bought two pieces from Rachel in the five years she'd known him and both had been really good pieces. She felt a lot easier about writing that cheque to Heather now and was sure that within the week she'd have enough money to cover it.

John and Rachel had idled a bit too long eating too much cake (if anyone can eat too much cake?) and had to hurry, they needed to be at St.John's, Escomb by eight at the latest to be let in and shown the whys and wherefores of their first night of "Glamping" in a Church.

They arrived and parked outside a little after eight and walked in. There were two other couples already there being shown around by a portly white bearded gentleman called "Ken", he was one of the local parishioners who had thought the scheme a great idea for "revitalising" the church, it would also help pay for the general upkeep.

"Sorry we're a bit late"

"No problem, I was just showing everyone I've set up a kettle and tea here just off the Aisle in the North Transept and you can sleep in the Nave on the fold out beds provided or in a small self contained sleeping bag if you've brought one."

"The beds will be fine"

"Right-ho, one last thing, there's a small door in the South Transept, first left and you'll see a Portaloo, its got a couple of ground lights to it, so you'll be fine if caught short in the "wee" small hours" Ken chuckled to himself and left the Glampers to it.

Brief introductions were made, there were three couples John and Rachel met Tim and Ann, both in their late 50's, thin lean academic types, Tim was making a study of Durham History so had leapt at the chance of staying over night in the Saxon Church, the other couple were Jem and Ralph, about the same age as they were, late 20's and glamping for much the same reason, the very low cost (£20 a night). Tim very much took over the evening's conversation, he was quite the font of all knowledge when it came to the Church and local history.

"Yes they believe the church was built in the 670's possibly the 690's but mostly from reused stones from the Roman Fort at Binchester, you can see some of the original Latin inscriptions in the walls."

"What's that?" John pointed to a large stone monument in the Chancel.

"Ah, that's something of an oddity" replied Tim, it's quite out of place with the rest of the church, a late medieval tomb carved from Nottinghamshire Alabaster, the finest and most expensive you could get at that time. You really must look at it in the morning. It's got a finely carved armoured figure on the cover stone, wearing a large peculiar cross on a chain and as you might expect from this period there is a faithful hound sat at his feet, but very unusually the whole edge of the top is carved with a large python or serpent swallowing his own tail"

"An Ouroboros!" exclaimed Rachel, she'd see the motif used in Victorian jewellery quite often to signify rebirth or everlasting life.

"Just so" replied Tim in a way that spoke strongly of him being in academia for most of his life.

"Whose tomb is it?" Jem asked, more to show willing in the ensembles conversation that out of real interest.

"That's the odd thing, its not for a local but a member of one of the great Durham noble families, one of the *Haliwerfolc,* Henry Neville of Raby and Bracepath, descended from the great Lord Ralph of the famous Battle of Neville's Cross." There was a blank expression from everyone but Rachel who now recalled the inscription on the ring.

"Was that in 1346?" she said.

"Yes that's the one, the good old Northumbrians gave David II a damn good thrashing! Shot him in the head with arrow he could never get out, gave him headaches for years afterwards." Tim snorted slightly with laughter at his own remarks, much to the deafening silence of everyone else.

"Of course" he continued "that was at the site of the Old Anglo Saxon Cross, but then there was a huge respect for those monuments, probably to do with the Cult of St.Cuthbert, they all revered him, doubly so after the Battle. It is said his *Corporax* was hoisted upon a spear and it was that that led them to victory, back then it was all very earnestly believed. That may indeed be why Henry Neville chose to be buried here, one of the oldest Anglo Saxon churches in the county, about the same period as St Cuthbert himself. In fact Henry was very devout, its said he had a personal relic of Cuthbert's which he had with him every moment of the day, some people say he was even buried with it."

"Can't we have look?" joked John

"There wouldn't be much point." replied Tim, "The whole tomb was refurbished in the late eighteenth century and they had to open it then and no finds were recorded. It was quite a habit of Antiquaries back then to go around the country finding excuses to open up the tombs of famous historical figures and root around for anything still left. In the very worst cases, particularly if the person were Royal they'd lop off a bit of hair and sell it mounted up as souvenirs, quite ghastly. Happily you wouldn't be allowed to do it today"

A little more chat and the three couples decided to turn in for the night, John and Rachel pulled out the beds and placed them side to side, snuggling up in the cold church and went to sleep.

The next morning they woke and the dimly lit church of the night before was illuminated by the bright golden light streaming in from the windows. Ken had arrived back to unlock the main door of the church and bring along foil wrapped bacon sandwiches and a full selection of just one cereal.

"Sleep well?"

"Yes fine thanks" replied John, though Rachel scowled at him. "You may have done but what was all that in the middle of the night?"

"All what?" John seemed genuinely surprised.

"You KNOW"

John didn't but it seemed fruitless to pursue the question with his bacon sandwich going cold on a table in the North Transept.

After breakfast they packed up their things but before leaving wanted to look properly around the Church and, of course take some more pictures on their phones.

They saw the old Roman inscriptions which had come from the robbed out stones from the Fort at Binchester, they looked at the carved Saxon detailing around the door ways and then they came to the alabaster tomb of Henry Neville. It was oddly placed, but just as Tim had described the evening earlier. Rachel took a couple of images of the top and a close up detail of the unusual shaped cross which Henry Neville was depicted wearing on a thick link chain. Beneath the serpent was a period inscription "Lett no man proffit from another at his lyfes peril"

At the base there was indeed a small eighteenth century addition, a plaque no more than eight inches long carved in fine white grey veined marble, each letter deeply carved and then highlighted in gold leaf,

"This tomb renovated by Thomas Thompson

Elvert's Bridge in the County of Durham,

7th August 1785

Requiescat In Pace"

Rachel took a photo of that too.

The holiday had been a welcome break, apart from John's libidinous night time wanderings (not all unwelcome) but every night Rachel could feel him pressing up against her and she had push him away to sleep.

Once back home Rachel took the ring and began photographing it properly to upload on Instagram, she included the details of the marks and the engraving but did not put a price.

Bill, who had helped identify the marks on the ring but had not seen the whole piece got in touch quickly, messaging Rachel and asking if he could drive up that afternoon and see it and asking how much it would be. She agreed that he could come and look at in person, but was still working out a price. He set off at once.

There was a knock on the flat door, "Come in Bill, it's open" Rachel called through. Bill was portly and struggled through the narrow corridor of their flat into the living room.

"Sorry it's so cramped and such a mess, we've just come back from holiday, take a seat I'll get the ring"

Bill sat down with considerable heft, straining the ingenuity of Ikea's chair designs to their absolute limit and eliciting an ominous creak, thankfully everything held firm.

"So where is he?" said Bill as he reached out for the ring with his left hand whilst thrusting the right into his waistcoat pocket like a reflex, withdrawing his jewellers loupe (magnifying glass) which was both achromatic and planar (colourless and free of distortion).

"Lovely, absolutely lovely" he muttered as he deftly turned the ring around just by the tips of his fingers with the loupe barely a inch or so away, scrutinising every little chip, scratch and blemish so he could to get the price down.

"So how much is it?"

Rachel paused, she had a cheque to cover so wanted a quick sale, but she knew Bill hadn't driven all the way up from

London to walk away empty handed.

"Five, it's got to be five"

Bill was stony faced and simply said "Four"

"No, no I can't do four" there was a slight pause as neither spoke, "but I'll split it with you"

Bill reached out his hand as he nodded and agreed "Four and half"

The deal was done and Rachel had just sold the ring for four and a half thousand pounds, a clear profit of four thousand and surely enough now for a deposit for the mortgage with everything else she and John had saved.

"Do you want a cheque now or shall I transfer the money?"

Rachel then realised when he'd said cheque that she hadn't written it from her business account but from their personal savings account in John's name. Can I get back to you this evening and we'll do a transfer then, I just need to get my husbands details, it will go into his account.

"Yes that's fine" replied Bill, he then fully relaxed with the ring safe in his pocket.

"I would have paid the five you know" he couldn't resist it and it was said with a wry smile. "Do you know how rare it is?"

Rachel had suspected as much but had made her profit out of it, "Go on then what is it." she sighed.

"This ring is from one of only two parcels of gold rings Thompson ever submitted for assay, I say Thompson, it was his daughter Jane that submitted them in his name after his untimely death in September 1785 from asphyxia, though Samuel had already made them and sold one, though prior to that he'd never worked in gold. It's odd because after that Jane is recorded as giving them all away, perhaps a last devotional act to her dead father, we'll never know for sure."

"Why Neville's Cross though?" Rachel asked

"Well it appears Samuel's brother Thomas, a stone mason by trade, had been asked to carry out some restoration work on the cross and a couple of other monuments that year and that had led Samuel to produce these commemorative rings with the distinctive Cross of St Cuthbert in his colours of blue and white, possibly as gifts for the benefactors of the work."

"Oh is that what the cross on the top is?"

"Yes, it was said that Cuthbert possessed a Gold pectoral cross, plain on a thick link chain, it was considered to be one of his great relics but was lost sometime at the end of the fifteenth century, probably stolen and melted down to make goodness knows what."

Rachel thanked Bill and showed him out and told him she'd send him the details for the Bank Transfer later that evening when John returned home.

It was around six and John came back in, looking thoroughly tired and agitated, "Good day at work?"

"Oh don't I've had a hell of a day, I think we've got rats at the council office."

"Rats? You've seen rats?"

"Well, no not seen but something kept pressing up beside my leg all afternoon under the desk, I'd have thought it was one of the lads having a laugh but no one else was in. Every time I ducked under the desk to look there was nothing there, bet the furry little beggars ran off, I've got pest control coming in the morning, they'll sort it out."

"Well sit down and I'll cook dinner I've got some good news"

Rachel explained about the ring and the cheque, John was alarmed she'd written it but felt much better when he heard about Bill's afternoon visit and the sale, four thousand would be a huge help.

"Here's the details for you, he can transfer the money tonight with any luck, it doesn't look as if the cheque's even been presented yet anyway"

Rachel emailed the details to Bill and he promised he'd do the transfer later that evening. Rachel and John decided on an early night.

It was about three in the morning that Rachel woke to hear a gasping noise form the other side of the bed, John's face had turned pale and his lips were blue and his arms were jerking as if something tight had been wrapped around chest and throat, squeezing the breath out him. She panicked and threw off the bed clothes, there was nothing there, but could she *feel* *something* there, thick and smoothly scaled and moving, pulsing, John felt his whole chest tighten again. By the time the paramedics came there was nothing they could do, they noted down a preliminary cause of death as Asphyxia, query unknown.

The next day Bill called only to hear the shocking news about John. He offered his deepest sympathies and apologised for intruding, he'd just wanted to say that he'd been out with friends yesterday evening and hadn't gotten home till about three in the morning and had remembered and done the transfer then, he was worried if might not have shown up but had hoped it had cleared immediately into John's account.

The Skeleton Clock

It was late October in 1935 and it had been a bad month all round. Rupert had gone to the sales at Christie's and Sotheby's but Hearst was in a buying mood. Everything he had wanted to buy for the shop had gone too far beyond his pocket to make a sensible return.

The fine pair of Hepplewhite Satinwood commodes had made over a hundred and forty guineas, the giltwood pier mirrors in the manner of Kent with their original candleholders in fine ormolu had been more, even the smaller pieces, like the run of Smart miniatures, which were always good dressing for the sides of an Adam fireplace or within a vitrine, had fetched over ten pounds each. Christmas was not that far away and he wanted something fresh in the shop for his clients, he determined his only option was to fire up his beloved Riley Kestrel and tour all the old dealers, through Hampshire and Wiltshire right down to Old "Taunton Tom" in Somerset and hope they'd all been buying well.

The trip was hit and miss, a Sheraton bookcase which needed work but had come straight out of Heckfield Place was secured for twenty five pounds and he felt sure it could be improved with some judicious additions of inlay and then there had been a small collection of passable Adam silver form Middlewick which was bought at six shillings an ounce, when he had seen the same sold to Hearst at fifteen. Rupert couldn't complain but he had not yet found that one special piece to draw in the attention of all and sundry into the shop and his last stop before journeying back was Old "Taunton Tom", though he thought if there was one rare piece to be found in the county, Tom would have it.

Rupert parked the Kestrel outside the shop, it was on Silver street, a small double bay fronted shop in black painted timbers with all manner of brass and copper utensils hanging above and stacks of country chairs, tables and curios on the pavement. If you thought the outside of the shop was cluttered the inside was far, far worse, the objects, some old, some bizarre, were piled high enough for there to be just one distinct path through the shop. Rupert scanned the piles as he walked through to the back of the shop, but knew well enough that this was all the day to day stock in trade of Tom's, the choicest pieces would be locked safely and separately at the back and you would only see those if you knew Tom.

He rounded the final corner made almost entirely of stacked rustic West Country hoop and stick back chairs, all rough and crusted with layers of red and green paint crumbling off them. He caught Old Tom's eye, as he sat in his usual high (and stained) wing back chair next to a low fire with a table and an open bottle beside him.

"Hello Mr Rupert, nice to see you 'ere again, you can ave them their h'old chairs for a shilling a piece, give me two and I'll even paint 'em for you"

The old man laughed and cackled at the joke. His good humour, though always well "lubricated" was infectious. Rupert smiled and sat down in the open rather nice Georgian cockpen chair facing him.

"This is nice Tom" Rupert stroked the delicate mahogany arms of the chair, "is it.."

"Gone, I'm afraid" Tom interrupted, "That an three others which goes with it are spoken for and off next Monday to a

68

man in Kent, but till then I sees no reason why you can't 'ave a sit of em"

Rupert was secretly disappointed, especially now he heard they were a set of four, still it showed Tom was still finding good things.

"So Tom I'm looking for something good and rare and interesting for the shop, what have got to show me, what have you got hidden away?"

Tom took out a long clay pipe and slowly filled and lit it with an ember lifted from the fire, he took three long draws to light it and billowed out a plume of grey smoke as he sat back in the well worn chair.

"Well, we 'ave just done the last of the local Hall owned by them old Carrows" He saw Rupert stir forward in his chair with a touch of excitement at the mention of a Hall being cleared.

"No, nothing for you to get too excited over Mr Rupert, they's been a bad lot for a long while, my Grandfather had all the plate off 'em near eighty year ago, right bad lot they was, he said. Then the good paintin's and the furniture not long after that, the place was run to rack and ruin when the old squire Sir George lost his son, then it was all nephews and cousins who didn't much care for the place, only what they could gets out of it. Last one now has upped and gone to the South of France they say, so I was called to clear it out before the place was sold"

Tom smiled "just a bit of spending money for his Lordship for when he see's em French ladies I reckons" he began chuckling again, tickled that he may be funding the lower ambitions of some of the highest in the land.

"So it's just odds and ends is it?"

"Now, I didn't say that did I Mr Rupert" The old man rose from his chair and placed his smouldering pipe down onto a china bowl next to the open brandy bottle on the table beside him. He shuffled past Rupert to the smaller room at the back and returned moments later carrying a clock on a wooden, possibly walnut, plinth under a large blown glass dome.

"Careful!" he called out as he half stumbled past Rupert, who rose to help him, but Tom had already found a place on a pile of old books to rest it safely.

"What 'bout that then?"

"It's a skeleton clock Tom."

"Yes, tis, but what be it made of I ask you?"

The light wasn't great in the shop, the fire and a couple of candles helped a little, Rupert took a closer look fully expecting it to be finely worked brass, he was surprised

"Ivory?"

"Yes Ivory as YOU say, I thought ye'd like that, I've not seen one of 'em before and look at the name." Tom pointed to a small engraved silver plaque fixed to the base, it read:

"To Sir George Carrow with the deep and sincere compliments of Thomas Lake, Clock and Watchmaker, newly moved to East Street, Taunton Tempus Metiri Hominem"

"A Taunton made skeleton clock, I thought they were all made in London by that firm in Clerkenwell, Smith and Sons, or the firms up in Birmingham and Liverpool?"

"No this one's as West Country as they come Mr Rupert, I reckon you'll never see its like again, fact I'm sure you won't"

"Alright, Tom how much?"

"Well seeing as it be you Mr Rupert, ten pounds cash, no h'arguments"

Rupert paused, it was a very fair price and not at all like Tom, he took another careful look,

"Including the dome Tom?"

Tom chuckled at the notion he would charge extra for the dome, but did think to do it next time.

"With the dome, I h'ain't no eyway man Mr Rupert"

They shook on the deal and Rupert packed it safely into the back of the Kestrel, he would take all the slow safe roads back to town on the return trip no matter how long it took.

The door of the Old Tom's shop closed, he sat back down in his chair and called up to his his long suffering wife Meg,

"It's gone."

Meg's reply came swiftly back

"Thanks be to God for that."

A week or two later Rupert had taken the clock to his horologist to clean it and get it working, in the meantime he would research the maker and the owner to see if it could add a little more value to his spectacular find.

He could already imagine it set in the front window on his good harewood side table, gleaming white and ticking away to the delight of passing interested customers. It would be the draw, exactly what he wanted, for the run up to Christmas.

Lake had seemed to be a good but workmanlike maker, the other clocks he could find were either country cased oak longcases or functional dial clocks, there seemed little else with the sheer work and complexity of this example, a clock it appeared from the plaque that he had seemed happy to give away.

He had slightly better luck tracing the life and career of Sir George Carrow to whom the clock had been given. He had served in the Napoleonic Wars as a youth and always seemed to be mentioned alongside some of the bloodier and more brutal actions. Upon his return to Taunton he was variously falling into trouble for duelling and brawling.

Rupert thought back to Old Tom's assertion that the Carrow's were "a right bad lot" and that seemed to be supported by the reports in some of the old papers. Why then, he wondered did Lake present him with the clock?

After some further research Rupert found a series of cuttings from the "Taunton Courier" which covered the period running up to the presentation of the clock (he had since discovered that Lake only moved to East Street in 1822 and that must be the approximate date of the clock).

Lake had a son and a daughter, the son followed him into his trade but the daughter, held to be one of towns great beauties, had suffered an attack reported in the March of 1822, it was not known who the assailant had been but she was reported to have been "cruelly and brutally treated" and had clearly not recovered from the incident when in June of the same year a Death Notice was published for her. It recorded that "Her loving Father had taken great pains to the neglect of all other business in her care until the end". This deeply saddened Rupert and made him all the more appreciative of the very fine work he had done that same year on the clock, had he undertaken the construction of it out of sheer grief he wondered?

Further on he found mention of George Carrow, well his son Robert aged 12, who was said to have been lost from his horse one morning in August. The horse had returned to Carrow Hall around ten and blood had been found on the saddle, it was presumed that Robert had struck something, possibly a branch and fallen from the horse which had then returned to the Hall stables, though extensive searches of the grounds and beyond could find no trace of him.

Things seemed to be going badly for Lake the clockmaker that month too, it was possibly the late heat of the summer, or a state of neglect brought on by the loss of his daughter months earlier, but his neighbours in Silver Street petitioned he be moved because of the "rank and vexatious stench arising from his workshop, worse than that of a tannery". It was after this that he moved to the new premises in East Street. Did he give the clock to Sir George Carrow because they had both lost children he wondered?

The next morning his restorer, Gerald rang and asked him to come and collect the clock, it had been cleaned and was now working, he said there was something in particular he wanted to show him.

The next morning Rupert drove down to Clerkenwell where Gerald's workshop was and entered,

"Morning, where is it then?"

Gerald a small thin man in his late forties with thinning black short hair and horn rimmed spectacles peered from behind the workshop's side door,

"Through here Rupert, I've got it all ready and running for you. Very rare piece this."

Rupert loved to hear that from any expert in their field, "I've never worked on one like it, dare say I never shall again, though it was the very devil to get a match for it."

"A match for what?" Rupert asked

"Why for the bone"

Rupert looked a little puzzled, "But it's Ivory isn't it?"

"You'd think it was but no, when I started cleaning it all and taking it apart I found it was bone, but very close grained, not at all as coarse and irregular as the bone you find on French prisoner of war work, where they've used cow or lamb bones, no this proved to be a real headache but I had a flash of inspiration."

"What?" asked a subdued Rupert.

"Well, I'm currently restoring this fine Tompion for one of the Heads of the Royal College of Surgeons and whilst he was here I asked him to take a look and see if he could identify the type of bone. He wasn't absolutely sure but felt from his experience a human bone would be a good alternative to replace the damaged and missing parts, all a bit gruesome I'm afraid but he obliged, said that he'd had an amputation and got a member of his staff to boil the leg down, took days apparently and the stench was horrendous, complaints from all the neighbours but once it was done and I'd cut the pieces out it was a near perfect match, so at least in one respect you do actually have a SKELETON CLOCK!" chortled Gerald.

Rupert was not laughing with him though, he was sat stunned and quiet but Gerald had yet one more thing to tell him.

"Oh and you see here, most odd on one of the main wheels there's a series of letters, you can't see them all at once when the clock is assembled and running, then its obscured by the other cogs and wheels so only one letter is ever showing at a time, in fact you'd be hard pressed to notice it even though its in plain sight, but I had to take it apart so saw the whole thing, I wrote it down on a piece of paper for you"

Gerald searched around in a workshop drawer for the pieces of paper and then handed it to him, in part it was the inscription on the plaque of the case "Tempus Metiri Hominem" but it continued "quia oculo ad oculum"

Translated it was "Time measured by man, an eye for an eye."

The clock was taken back to the shop and quickly sold to the next customer in, it had not been placed in the window. It was described as being in the style of the French Prisoner of War work carved from animal bone at Norman's Cross and it fetched £50, though the plinth it was one did have a small mark where it appeared a small plaque had been removed.

Ebhart's Receipt.

Rob had spent the morning at his desk in the Archaeology department tiding and packing everything up before he left the University, his brief one year contract had come to an end and nothing else was waiting for him. He knew to get on and get another more secure position, perhaps at another University or a Museum, he had to buckle down and find a significant piece of research to do and finally think about getting his PhD.

He stacked two cardboard boxes, full of papers, books, odd bits of stationary and a couple of well stained mugs, the last twelve months hadn't come to much. He lifted them up and took them down to the car. As he locked the boot after trying to close it twice (it was an old car falling apart the seams) it occurred that he might just as well get one last free lunch, so wandered into the Student's dining hall where happily members of staff ate without charge.

Rob gathered a selection of the most deeply fried foods that he could from the impressive choice of burgers, dogs, chips and hash browns on offer, determined to save the price of dinner that evening too, piling his plate as high as he dare without attracting attention, then took his canteen tray to find a quiet table. He saw John was sitting alone and walked to join him.

"Good afternoon Rob, not often we see you here in the canteen with us mere mortals" came a sarcastic tone as he approached.

"It's my last day John."

John had clearly forgotten his old roommates imminent departure,

"Oh Rob, sorry, I could lie, but I've clean forgotten, well, anyway all the very best for whatever's next. Out of interest what is next?"

Rob had started to tuck into the mountain of food in front of him, so chewing the last mouthful would give him a few seconds to consider his reply, as he really didn't want to say he hadn't got a clue.

As he finished slightly nodding his head and pointing at his chewing mouth with the tines of his fork, he swallowed and replied

"I'm going to do a bit of archival research in town, thinking of doing something current and relevant, the overlooked role of slavery in the industrial growth of England, or something along those lines" as he was making it up it began to sound like a good idea to himself.

John nodded, "Well, that does sound interesting. I think I can help point you in the right direction, there's a group of documents and periodicals that I was looking through last year in Richmond, they mentioned a number of slave auctions I think? You'd have to go through them in person, but that is the great thing, no one's digitised the local archives yet so anything you find will probably be pretty new to most people."

Rob made a note of the archive address that John gave him and proceeded to polish off the rest of his enormous lunch, hoping that there may be some work to be getting on with after all.

Rob got home about five and started making dinner for Anna, but not himself. He was still full from the enormous deep fried excesses of lunch. They'd both met doing Archaeology at Winchester six years ago, but whilst he'd stayed in straight academia she'd been taken by the finds side of it at the summer digs they used to assist on and was now a full time material conservationist. Thankfully Anna's skills were in constant demand, something John was grateful for, especially now his employment had come to an end. He heard the key turn in the lock of the flat's door as he deftly chopped an onion.

"Hi there, I'm home" came Anna's voice as she walked through dropping two large bags in the hall, "everything ok?"

"Yes, I'm just doing you dinner, but I'm not having any, I filled up in the dining hall as a sort of last supper"

"Oh don't get down" she walked up behind him and slipped a comforting arm around his waist, "Something will turn up" she kissed him lightly on the neck.

"It may have done already, I saw John at lunch and he's put me onto a bit of archival research which may turn into something. I'm going to call through and see if I can make an appointment to go up next week."

"Well," laughed Anna, "that means I've got you all to myself this weekend" Rob didn't finish preparing dinner.

A week later found Rob wading through the depths of the local archives in a civic building which had the charm of an abattoir and horrid strip lighting throughout, it was a Kafkaesque nightmare in waiting.

John had been right, nothing had been digitised, there were banks of shelves and filing cabinets in the dimly lit basement, together with a vintage microfiche reader which looked like a monitor he had seen as a boy on the deck of Liberator from Blake's 7.

He took down another box of papers from the shelves and opened to find copies of the local gazettes from the 1750's and 60's. There were indeed chilling mentions of auctions which included slaves but nothing more substantive, certainly nothing to start a Phd, then he noticed one large notice for a sale

"Notice of an Auction of the entire contents of the premises of the late Captain Eynsworth and Mr George Fell's China Works near Little Marble Hill, Richmond, 3rd September 1765"

He thought it was odd as he'd never heard of a China Works in Richmond and it might, he thought, be interesting. He noted it down and would show it to Anna when he got home. She was a really into her 17th and 18th century material culture. He continued through the dimly lit and oppressive archive for the rest of that day, it was a fairly soul destroying experience and he left with little expectation that it would bear worthwhile fruit.

He got back to Winchester around eight and Anna was in and a dinner cooked.

"How did it go?"

Rob just waved his hand back and forth with a comic sad face,

Anna consoled him "Oh, sorry love, I know you'd hoped something might come of it."

"Well, there was this." Rob pulled the note he'd made of the auction advert in the gazette to show Anna, she took it and as she read her eyes widened. He could tell at once, "Is, is it anything?"

Anna had done some reconstructive work on a group of delft (tin glazed) pottery shards, the year before. Wasters from a previously unrecorded workshop that had been found in a pit excavated at dig in Lambeth prior to the site being turned over for development. She remembered the excitement there had been about it and had subsequently got quite into her British pottery and porcelain as a result.

"Rob, this could be an unknown London factory, there are only five known. I mean I don't want to get your hopes up. You've got to do a lot more digging and it really could come to nothing, but an unrecorded porcelain factory, that would be quite big find, it could certainly do for a PhD."

Rob, with little else to do over the coming weeks, really threw himself into his research. He went through all the rent books and insurance policies he could find of the period for the Richmond area, particularly around Little Marble Hill. Anna had told him that all the known London factories, Chelsea, Bow, Limehouse, Vauxhall and Isleworth had been situated on the Thames or on one it's tributaries. He concentrated on those areas and found an old Sun Insurance policy for "Eynsworth and Fell China Works, 1000 sq feet one workshop and kiln, Little Marble Hill, Richmond £250"

Some of the other working factories were on a far greater scale and size, some insured for £600 or £1000 so initially Rob was worried that whilst they may have intended to make porcelain they didn't actually achieve it which would have been a bit of a damp squib. Still he persevered with his researches, he was too far into it now.

Captain Eynesworth was proving an elusive figure for someone with such a distinctive name. Rob had gone through both the military and naval records available online without any success.

George Fell proved far more obliging and there was good paper trail for him, prior to 1763 and his partnership with Eynesworth he had been a successful Chemist in the City of London. He had been born in Bristol to a Quaker family and had social connections with both the Champion and Cooksworthy families, though there seems to have been no traceable direct business link. He was known to have met regularly with Richard Champion during his time in London in the early 1760's, though back then Champion had no involvement in the production of porcelain (he was later to return to Bristol and run a china works there). Perhaps it was possible Fell had influenced him in that direction?

A surviving notebook held in the Wellcome collection dating from around 1750-63 showed that Fell had a fascination for experimentation which went in tandem with his business as a Chemist, keenly pursuing attempts at working out various secret formulae, hard paste porcelain being amongst them with various degrees of success, well mostly degrees of failure.

A month into his work Rob had worked out, within a quarter of a mile or so, where the porcelain factory should be located, if it indeed had successfully produced porcelain. It was still fairly open ground, lots of big gardens and fields to dig in, there was a particularly open green area around the "Stranger's Hall" which had been built in 1766.

When he investigated the Hall further to see who's permission he needed to dig an exploratory trench or two he discovered it had been built by George Fell, "to freely assist and accommodate any and all immigrants in want coming into the City of London", clearly a good work coming from his strong Quaker roots but it was surely more than likely that he had erected it on the old factory site? All Rob had to do was get the permissions and pray that there was something left to find. In the meantime he would try to pin the tail of the identity of Captain Eynesworth's donkey and think on where he could get the funding for the dig.

That evening, at home in Winchester, after dinner, Anna told Rob he better send his best suit to the dry cleaners.

"I haven't got the time or the money to take you out this weekend love."

"Well you better have the time to take yourself out."

Anna replied and handed Rob an invitation,

"and you better go given all the favours I had to call in to get you that."

It was a crisp card invitation printed in beautiful copperplate for the Ceramics Circle AGM, though he learnt it was more of a formal bun fight than an academic study day.

"Why've you got me this?" He asked, Anna had always been the more intelligent of the two.

"Firstly you can discreetly enquire about research into any new factory sites that's being done and secondly you might just find someone interested and wealthy enough to fund your dig."

Rob quietly smiled at how clever he had been to marry someone so much cleverer than himself.

The evening of the AGM, Rob travelled up to London in his best suit to one of the Livery Company Halls which had been hired for the evening, it was a plush event and clearly some very wealthy people were members. A colleague of Anna's who she'd worked with the year earlier on the pottery shard conservation met him at the door, Jim, it was he, as a senior member of the circle, who had been able to get Rob a ticket.

"My dear boy do come in. Lovely to meet you, Anna said you were starting to get interested in English porcelain, well the more young members we can rope in the better. Do come through."

The room was sumptuous and some very well turned out figures were mingling beneath a series of impressive Osler chandeliers, which were softly lighting the numerous murmuring conversations below. Rob helped himself to a glass of champagne and a canapé as Jim began to introduce him around.

After about half an hour Rob had met half the people in the room but hadn't really been able to hold an intelligent conversation with any of them, well not without mentioning his research and he certainly wasn't going to do that. That was until he met Roderick, or Ricky as he much preferred to be called. Unlike the immaculately turned out majority Ricky was wearing bright yellow trousers, a loose but well tailored denim jacket and a smart pair of shoes from Lobb which had cost half what Rob had earned in the previous year. He was in his late forties thin and very well tanned, almost brown and with a polished soft public school voice, the plum was there but the stone had been removed and he commanded the casual confident demeanour of the very well bred and the very well heeled.

"So, why have you wandered into the lion's den old chap?" Ricky gestured to the surrounding crowd of members around them.

"Well my wife got me the invite, she did a bit of work with Jim last year and I became interested in the porcelain side of it" Rob lied "You know early English and in particular the newly discovered factories in and around London, Isleworth isn't it?"

Ricky smiled, "Well Isleworth is the last one we've found up to now, but there's so much work being done and so many pots that we really have no idea where they were made. It's one of my interests, I buy odd pots and analyse them, hoping to put them into groups and then of course you hope one day someone digs up a shard and bingo! You've got a new factory and everyone's in the money."

"Money?" Rob replied "How do you make money out of it?"

"I'm not really sure I should tell you." teased Ricky, "No, its quite simple. If you discover a new factory a new class of wares, all of sudden some nameless faceless pot becomes desirable. It happened with Isleworth, people bought pieces for hundreds, then found they were a brand new factory and sold them for thousands. Its happened a few times over the years, attributions, particularly for the early experimental wares change a lot, much more frequently than you think. Look if you're really interested I can show you a selection of pieces I've still yet to identify, I'm at home for the morning tomorrow?"

Rob thought he had found just the man he wanted to talk to and agreed to be at Ricky's house in Spitalfields for ten the next morning. His mission accomplished he helped himself to one more glass of champagne for the road and slipped quietly away.

The next morning Rob found himself standing before an impressive grey brick town house in Spitalfields, it hadn't been turned into flats, Ricky clearly owned the whole thing, which Rob thought must run to two or three million at the very least. He approached the finely panelled door, painted in a rich period dark green and made two confident 'knocks' with the heavy cast scroll Georgian brass knocker.

"Morning, do come through" Ricky ushered him along the wide hall to a door on his immediate right.

"It's not quite Denis Severs house I'm afraid, I must have my widescreen and induction hob, but I keep this room as period as possible."

It was a fine early Georgian panelled room with a central marble fireplace and sash windows with the original shutters folded back. As far as Rob could tell all the furnishings were period eighteenth century, two wing back chairs and a pad foot walnut folding table open before the fire with silver cast candlesticks upon it.

"Come over here" Ricky was standing in front of a large

mahogany cabinet with solid doors, when he opened them Rob couldn't quite recall seeing so much blue and white porcelain at once.

"Here are all the uncategorised pieces I've found over the years" Ricky explained, "Each shelf has one or two different groups of wares on it based on the similarities of the glaze and composition of the body, some of them have ten or twenty pieces in each group, others have five to ten and then here on the top shelf we get the real oddities, a handful of single items we just can't place, this one's my favourite."

He handed Rob a teapot painted in underglaze blue with a biblical scene of a man holding a dagger and an Angel flying down towards him,

"It's Abraham sacrificing his son" commented Ricky, "But the real interest is the base, here let me take the cover and you can turn it over"

Ricky took to foliate painted cover with its small daisy knop from Rob and let him turn it over. Underneath was a small open crescent mark, a copy surely of Worcester, but beside it, scratched into the body of the porcelain were the letters

"Pb 6-17"

"This one's a bit of mystery, no one's figured it out yet. I suspect the Pb may indicated a lead glaze and the numbers different test firings, 6-1, 6-2, 6-3 and so on, though why they would do it on such large and finished wares is beyond me."

Rob could see beyond just the financial attraction of

discovering a new factory and making money from it, this was clearly Ricky's passion. He took the plunge and took him into his confidence, only holding back the precise names and locations, he explained fully his situation and what he was hoping to get out of it.

Ricky sat back in one of the wing chairs and thought for a minute, all the time looking intently at Rob, he then lunged forward with his hand outstretched and simply said

"You're on, I'll back you, let's dig the whole bloody place up!"

Preparations began in earnest for the dig on what Rob believed to be the factory site, the local University would assist and be the formal route for obtaining the permissions but Ricky was footing the not inconsiderable bill. By now Rob had taken him entirely into his confidence and the two men were trying to track down more about the seemingly elusive Captain Eynesworth.

"Look I've got a friend who's a military historian, met him years ago when I was trying to work a regimental inscription on a large Lowestoft mug. Give him a call, he's sound as a pound, maybe he can point us in the right direction."

David dealt in Militaria and was fanatical about his subject, loving the research side of things as much as the objects themselves. Rob gave him a call and asked if he had come across a Captain Eynesworth, anytime around the 1760's.

"No, I don't think I have but the name's familiar, just let me think, you don't know his first name do you, it's not Richard by any chance?"

Rob got excited, "Yes, yes it is, do you know him?"

"Yes and I know now why you couldn't find any reference for him as a Captain, well I do if its the same person I'm thinking about. There was a diary published back in the 1880's of a MR Richard Eynesworth, a transcript of a mid eighteenth century document which mentioned, amongst other things his time serving abroad as a mercenary in the seven years war, he was never a British officer. Look I haven't read it for ages but I'll dig it out and post it to you as soon as I can, though do send it back when you're finished."

"Yes, yes, certainly, happy to." Rob replied.

The diary was posted to Rob's flat and Anna was in when it arrived. It was a Saturday so she opened it and took out the slim crimson pamphlet, rather than a full book and settled down to read it before Rob got back, she put Radio 3 on and sat down in the most comfortable chair in the flat with a hot cup of tea beside her.

The diary or autobiography, it seemed to read as both, was written by Richard Eynesworth, though that had been later discovered by the compiler of the text, the pages of the diary originally being unsigned in any way, which might, Anna thought account for their frankness. It ran from the late 1740's upto 1765. It appeared Eynesworth came from a noble but impoverished family in the North of England and he had travelled to London to establish himself as a "Physick" or Doctor, though it appears his "patent nostrums" whilst selling well to the poorer and needier inhabitants of the city also caused a deal of illness and pain themselves. He recounts how he was called out to attend a sick child of a Magistrate only to administer one of his concoctions to fatal effect.

It was later found by a qualified Physician to contain both arsenic and mercury in "unsound quantity". Before charges could be levelled Eynesworth fled for the Continent where he attempted to make his fortune in various unsuccessful fashions. It was in the spring of 1760 that he found himself a paid mercenary in the services of Prince Ferdinand of Brunswick-Wolfenbuttel, preparing to do Battle in Warburg.

In his own words he "feared for his own life to such a degree" that he intended to flee back to England by any means necessary, in doing so he ended up in completely the wrong place during the Battle and was put in a situation where he had to engage a small French scouting party who were ambushing a small detachment of his own regiment carrying messages, it was that or be captured himself.

The engagement was successful. Though driven purely by selfish motives he had earned the admiration of his officers and the eternal gratitude of one of the men he helped save, a native German Johann Ebhart.

The evening after the Battle Eynesworth recounts how Ebhart came to him and wished to repay the debt, first though he pressed him on what he intended to do, was it to stay in Germany or return to England? Eynesworth assured him that if he could assist him to return to England that would be thanks enough. That reassured Ebhart and he began to speak in a much quieter tone as he passed Eynesworth a small leather pouch with a thick chord around it, gesturing for him to tie around his neck and tuck it safely beneath his shirt.

Ebhart whispered to him,

"I was, before being called to serve in the Prince's regiment in the employ of his father King Charles I at the castle in Furstenburg. I served for eleven years in the castle manufactory as one of the many assistants to the factory Master Johann Georg von Langen. (nb it had been the fashion for Princes and Nobles throughout Continental Europe to attempt to establish their own porcelain works as a status symbol and to supply luxury objects for the Court).

The receipt (recipe) of the porcelain body was a closely guarded secret but von Langen could not and would not do all the work himself. We were separately asked to bring different loads of clays and numerous other materials to the workshops where the body (porcelain clay) was prepared. I carefully watched and noted all the parcels over the following years, realising some of the ingredients asked for were simple done as a ruse, whilst others were stored up to make the right quantity at different times. If you swear to keep this secret and not use it yourself to make porcelain until you return to England, I shall give you a copy of receipt to repay my debt."

Eynesworth duly swore an oath, though had there been an opportunity to sell it there and then for a good price he would have done so. He kept the small leather pouch tightly about his neck at all times.

His misfortune only three weeks later was to be shot in the right shoulder. It was not the injury, which was quickly and properly treated, that was the problem but the charring of the shot which had clipped the edge of the leather pouch having worked its way up to just under the shoulder belt of his uniform.

Ebhart had sadly departed back to Furstenburg a week earlier and Eynesworth had no way of finding him during his convalescence. He unwrapped the paper he had been given to see that two full ingredients on the list had been obliterated and he rued not taking the precaution of making a copy or memorising it. Still it was only two ingredients, perhaps with a little experimentation, putting him in mind of his days as "Phyisck" he could work it out himself.

When the wound healed he made his way slowly back to England through another series of misadventures, finally arriving in London in the May of 1763. It was then, in trying to procure the ingredients mentioned on the list and others to add as tests that he met the Quaker chemist George Fell.

At first it seems Fell supplied Eynesworth with raw materials on credit, then when it got to such a large debt (a figure of £100 is noted down) it appears Eynesworth and Fell went into partnership, discharging Eynesworth's individual debts to the firm. It is now that they sort a small premises on the river, far enough form prying eyes, the site near Little Marble Hill in Richmond.

From there on the account is more a workmanlike diary, with notes of ingredients tried as additions to Ebhart's receipt, though Fell appears to have taken over the entire experimental side of the business being the more qualified of the two men, with Eynesworth taking care of day to day matters of the supply of materials and labour, which they appeared to have kept to a minimum. Like so many trying to find the secret of true porcelain they seemed to have struggled bitterly, even with a the near complete formula from Ebhart.

It was a full year later on the 8th June 1764 that the entries in the diary change, rather than simple ingredients Eynesworth noted:

"Fell had a grave accident whilst mixing the final elements of the body so much so that we believed it spoiled. He was immediately rushed back home and tended carefully by his family until recovered. I thought to discard the badly tainted mix but with little else to do had it made up and fired in case any seconds should be produced that might sell"

The entry for three days later was simply the word

"Success!"

Thereafter the factory must have grown rapidly, Anna thought, as the diary now reverted simply to a series of notes over the following weeks by Eynesworth of staff newly employed at the factory, interspersed with notes of "Successfully fired". All of this as Fell was still recovering form his accident.

"Two men, one wife and child (French)"

"One maiden and young child (French)"

"Successfully Fired"

"Three men (West Indies)"

"One man and wife (German)"

"Successfully Fired"

etc.

Anna broke the excellent news to Rob that there was now definite proof that the two men had at least succeeded in making the porcelain body, now it was down to him to actually find it. Really nothing less than a kiln and a pit full of factory wasters would do but they both felt very close to an important discovery, something that could alter their lives for ever.

Two weeks had passed and though the weather had turned foul and cold it couldn't have dampened Rob, Anna and Ricky's spirits. Everything had been arranged and the dig was to commence on Monday once the geophysics had gone over the open gardens around the site at Stranger's Hall that weekend. They all met at Ricky's Spitalfields town house to discuss the best plan of action, there had been a strong response which Ricky was hopeful may be the kiln and then fainter signals of perhaps a pit and a wall. They had the volunteers from the University and a small digger so decided to put in three trenches. It was exciting and just like the digs Rob and Anna had met on.

The weather had got worse, fine persistent rain and a chill wind which whipped briskly off the river, but everyone was excited and the first trench went in. Unfortunately what they had hoped may be a factory wall, maybe to a potting room, was evidently the remains of an old World War II bomb shelter, with modern stamped bricks and concrete footings. Rob was hoping that all the signals they had gotten weren't going to end up being nothing more than later works and structures.

By mid morning the second trench went in and it was much better news, after a foot or so of digging evidence began to emerge of a single round brick bottle kiln, a ring of discoloured Georgian bricks. Ricky congratulated Rob but reminded him it was all still circumstantial at this stage, they really needed to find the porcelain factory wasters.

The first day ended with a continuing excavation of the kiln, they would put in a third and fourth trench tomorrow either side of it to hopefully locate the dump of kiln wasted fired wares.

In the meantime Rob had vigorously continued on the paper trail to trace what became of the two men after the advertised Auction of the factory in the September of 1765. He had well established that Fell had constructed the Stranger's Hall on the factory site just a year later and had then undertaken to almost exclusively dedicate himself to charitable works, to the extent that he sold his Chemists shop in the City too. Eynesworth however seemed to have left no trace at all.

Given he had styled himself a Captain on his return to England when he was a mere mercenary Rob suspected he would not have been beyond changing his name altogether if he was set on another money making scheme as he had appeared to be utterly without principal and he could see from the final entries in his diary that both he and Fell had a badly falling out some weeks before the China works was put up for sale.

"Fell recovered, returned to the factory today and I shared with him our great success in the firing of a good and true body though he was most unsettled within his own mind upon it."

The following entry was the last one in the diary and only a couple of weeks prior to the Auction of the chattels of the business:

"He (Fell) came into the finishing shop against my instruction to the workmen and began feverishly marking all the pots to be fired the next day. I took him from there myself when called and bid him not to return until the firing that night. I shall deal with the matter finally then."

The next morning at the dig it was only Rob and Anna, Ricky had a series of meetings and was leaving them to it now, standing in a wet field for hours watching a digger and a handful of Archaeology students had not been his idea of fun.

The first trench, where the smaller anomaly had shown on the geophysics turned up trumps, as the bucket of the digger took of a thin layer of dark soil and almost perfect round of white broken porcelain appeared. They began at once to carefully clear the pieces, putting it into trays which Anna would hopefully go through to piece everything together to get partial pots.

After a few hours of digging and several dozen trays of pieces had been sent to the nearby tent where Anna had set up the finds tables Rob went to see how she was getting on, hoping to see a partially completed teapot, tea bowl, anything he could take to show Ricky for all his trust in funding them.

As he entered the tent he could hear Anna snapping at one of the students "not there!" and throwing her hands up over her face in sheer frustration.

"What is it love?"

Anna slumped and turned and said "This is impossible! I've been on digs like this before and you always get the pots thrown into the pit, some break in two, some smash but you always get smaller and larger shards which you can sort through and match up with patience."

"So?" said a perplexed Rob,

"Well look! Look for yourself!" Anna ran her fingers through the porcelain fragments in one of the plastic trays in front of her, it almost dropped through her fingers like sand.

"It's been pulverised, all of it, deliberately pulverised. There's the odd small, very small piece where you can see a bit of leaf in blue, or the edge of a flower but no one would ever be able to piece any of this together, not even if they had years. Though it's odd too, sifting through it all I've yet to find anything which shows signs of being misfired in the kiln, it all seems to have been perfectly fired and glazed then utterly smashed?"

Although Rob had definitely found the factory, he hoped for a row of fully and partly made up pots to reveal to the world, this seemed only a half a victory for his efforts and he knew Ricky would be devastated too. But then a call came over the radio which made things rather worse. He was called back to where they were excavating the pulverised kiln wasters.

One of the more senior University diggers Moira, who was overseeing the volunteer students came up to him.

"Rob I'm sorry we've got human remains, we'll have to get Tracey in to excavate them and take them off for analysis."

"Where are the remains?" asked Rob.

Moira took him over to the pit of factory wasters. The students had cleared off the first layer and had now exposed a series of tightly packed bones within the porcelain shards, shiny and white they had all, it seemed, been neatly arranged and stacked around in a circle, with the skulls seemingly placed in the middle. It was a gruesome and unsettling sight. Rob collapsed a little and stepped away to compose himself.

Tracey was called in and whilst Anna continued to run the finds side of it, the focus had shifted to the careful removal and classification of the "bone pit" as the students had now named it. It went down in all about six feet and the bones were packed in tightly between layers of the pulverised china, though they had been arranged with deliberate care. Curiously at the very bottom was a complete skeleton, not like the stacked and assembled bones above it and it had a small wooden box placed upon it which was immediately sent to Anna for conservation.

Anna took the box, a simply pine one about eight inches square and began to ease the lid open which had been only lightly pinned shut, as if someone were expecting it to be opened. She set the lid carefully to one side and found a thick leather bag inside packed around with chalk dust to keep out any moisture from the surrounding soil. The bag had still deteriorated somewhat and began to fall away as she lifted it out. As the thick brittle pieces of hide fell away she was surprised to see a complete blue and white teapot in a perfect state of preservation. She quickly took some images on her phone and mailed them to Rob. She cleaned any residue gently from the surface and examined the base, it had an open blue crescent mark and had been scratched into the body of the clay, in a somewhat irregular, trembling hand "M 13-50"

Rob called Ricky and sent him the images of the teapot,

"Rob can you bring it around tomorrow? It looks the twin of mine I'd love to compare them."

"Sure I'll get Anna to bring it along and we'll see you around 12.00, great. I've just got to call into the University first to get Tracey's analysis of the bones, I'll bring that too."

The following morning Rob left Anna to carefully pack the teapot and take it over to Ricky's, he'd meet her there after visiting the University's Osteology department.

When he arrived Tracey welcomed him in and got him to put on a forensic cover all to view the rooms where the bones had been assembled into skeletons.

"Quite a mix you've got her Rob". Her jolly tone undercut the macabre sight of rows of partially assembled skeletons on the steel mortuary tables in front of him.

"So far we've partially or fully assembled about eight people, with that many to go again, I can say we've got a fair old mix, probably nine men of varying age, three women and the skulls of four juveniles, so sixteen in all excluding the body in the bottom of the pit found with the box, the one sealed in by the jumbled jigsaw of bones above it."

"Any clue to say how or why they they died yet?"

"Hang on, we're only just starting to put them all together, though I can say that the complete skeleton from the bottom pit did have a visible musket wound to the right shoulder, though the bone grown around small fragments of bedded shot seem to suggest it was something he, it was a male, recovered from, so not the cause of death. There appear to be signs of charring on all the remains."

"Thanks Tracey, well keep me up to date, I must dash off now."

Rob arrived at Ricky's a little later than planned, Anna had already arrived with the teapot from the excavations and it had been placed next to Ricky's mystery pot from his own collection, they were two identical peas in a pod.

"Rob, look they are twins!" Ricky full of awe and delight turned them both around, feeling the glaze and hard porcelain body, both had been marked with a Worcester style mark but were now clearly, as the dig had demonstrated, the currently only extant wares from the newly discovered factory of Eynesworth and Fell in Richmond.

"I'd still love to know what these scratched marks in the base mean though, I doubt now, seeing the two together identical in every respect, that they do correspond to different types of body or glaze."

This was Anna's first time seeing the two together and as the brighter of the three she looked at the scratched in inscriptions and had a flash of brilliance.

"Fell, Fell was quite a devoted Quaker wasn't he?"

"Yes." replied Rob.

"Well don't these look like Bible verses to you?"

Both men gave each other a quick glance as if to say hell why didn't we think of that, but then Ricky reached over to a shelf and took a book from it and handed it to Anna.

"Here, you should do the honours Anna."

The first inscription was Pb 6-17, Anna searched through the book of Proverbs

"Haughty eyes, a lying tongue and hands that shed innocent blood"

The second , M 13-50 Anna turned to correct verse in Matthew,

"and will throw them into the furnace of fire; in that place there will be weeping and gnashing of teeth."

The dig was concluded and no more pieces from the newly discovered factory appeared. It seemed that after Eynesworth's disappearance Fell closed the factory and seemingly destroyed every vessel made, except for the two surviving teapots.

Tracey finished her analysis of the bones and found the skeletons had come from people all over Continental Europe and three of the male skeletons were from even further afield, America or the West Indies.

Rob said nothing when the work was published but they seemed to match the descriptions of the unskilled refugee workers in Eynesworth's diary.

The last piece of the puzzle was when Ricky sent his own Richmond teapot to be analysed. It had much a similar formula to some of the porcelains made in central Germany at the same time but with some odd additions, in particular it was found to be peculiarly rich in Iron.

The Broken Lanx

Chris had got up at an ungodly hour, woken by an old two bell alarm clock he picked up in a job lot. No matter how loudly he set the ringer on his iphone it just wouldn't wake him.

A week earlier he'd gone to London to see which pitch he was getting and had trouble parking his car then. Despite that he had found a small bit of street in Ladbroke Gardens but knew he'd need to be there no later than about half five to be sure of a space. After showering and throwing on some clothes, then loading the boxes and the trolley into the back of the car he set off, in the blackness of the early morning, to the sounds of Kasabian on the car's cd player, turned up loud to keep him awake.

He got into Kensington and Chelsea in good time, there was little else on the roads so early. Having parked up he opened the boot and stacked the boxes onto the trolley. He wheeled them down a couple of streets, nearly losing the lot on an obliquely set errant paving stone, but gathered himself and made it safely to where his new pitch was marked, a little way down on Westbourne Grove, just off the main drag of Portobello.

It had been the nagging of a few local dealers he knew that had tipped him over into taking the plunge to stand out weekly in London, it was a fair old trip from Bridport but it might just be worth it.

He started unpacking the boxes onto the bare cheap wooden trestle table provided, he shook the legs at least twice before daring to put anything valuable on it, though it seemed sturdy enough. As he unpacked his stock from reams of bubble wrap the Sun started to come up over the roof tops opposite and the bright rays skated across the dark cold quiet roads.

Very soon after he'd laid out a couple of tea sets and a pile of flatware, another dealer, slightly older than himself in a sports jacket, well worn jeans and trainers, infused in every part with the vague menace of a lone football hooligan, swaggered up to him with his tea in one hand and started picking up everything on the table and then banging it roughly down.

"Morning, first time here?" said Vic, a dealer whose family had been buying and selling up and down Portobello Road for as long as anyone had ever thought to do it.

"Yeah, thought I'd give it a go" replied Chris as he continued to unpack the smaller items from his last box, placing them in a lockable display case he'd brought along for safety's sake.

"How much you got on the three piece?" Vic casually gestured with the brim of his polystyrene cup, spilling a little Tea on to the pavement as he did so, the very Georgian silver tea set that he'd just banged down on the table.

"Six and a half"

"What's it weigh?"

"Thirty four and a half all in" ("all in" was meant to include anything on the set which was not made of silver, the ivory insulators in the handle or the carved wooden finial on the

104

cover).

"That the best?" said Vic, the standard reply of any dealer.

"I'll do six for cash"

Vic put his tea down on Chris' table and reached into the front pocket of his jeans taking out a thick wad of fifty pound notes, he quickly flicked through and handed the cash over, "check that" he barked.

Chris did and then wrapped the teapot, milk jug and sugar basin carefully from all the bubble wrap he'd thought to bring with him. He then stuffed it unceremoniously into an old Sainsbury's carrier bag, they were starting to get like gold dust around the fairs and markets with everyone going plastic free.

"Thanks"

The two men were slightly more relaxed with one another now blood had been spilt and the first deal done. Vic was very much the "Top Boy" in the market, or at least that's how he saw it, due to his family's long standing. His own father had a stall just after the War and only retired the year previously. Vic started to offer unsolicited advice to the new face, partly to establish the pecking order but also to genuinely help out. He may have looked as though he'd have beaten you up in dark alley but he had a heart of gold and knew what it weighed down to the last gram.

"You'll sell most your decent trade stuff now, before 8.00 am, then there's a bit of a lull and the punters start arriving for all the odds and ends, but if it's a sunny day and doesn't rain you can do alright from the bit and bobs. Oh and if it's your first time here you're bound to get a visit from 'Big Mick' he does all the scrap flatware"

Vic pointed to a pile of forks and spoons on Chris' table as he spoke, for which Chris felt quite aggrieved, they were, he thought worth far more than the scrap price of the silver.

"There he is" Vic pointed to a large, very large, rough looking figure walking down the street. He was quite the stand out spectacle and not all what you would expect an antiques dealer to look like, more the look of a menacing Geoff Capes.

Over six foot and with long grey hair and a sergeant majors moustache. He wore a large tattered serge great coat, the type new romantics had favoured in the 80's and rifled through their grandfather's wardrobe to find. Under that was a black moleskin waistcoat with watch and chain and a slightly ruffled thick smock like white shirt, open at the neck and tied with a neckerchief or scarf. He had on a pair of well worn cords and a thick soled pair of enormous hobnail boots laced up to the ankle, carrying what looked like a large shopping bag, but it was worn and stained and made of thick old, very old, leather, the sort a plumber might had carried their tools in.

"He can get anything in that bloody bag" Vic said "My Dad swears he hasn't changed a bit in all the years he's known him, old now and old then. Look I'll come back later and see how you've got on, and watch out for 'Big Mick', he'll probably have something for you" Vic just grinned and left.

It had started to get busy in the few shorts minutes they'd been talking and more dealers were crowding around the pitch, picking up pieces left, right and centre, barking out "how much?!" and "best price?!" It was like a feeding frenzy and

Chris struggled to keep up with all the deals whilst maintaining an eagle eye on his stock, but as quickly as it had happened it all died down. Half the table was emptied in five minutes and Chris had sizeable roll of notes in his pocket. Then shortly after 'Big Mick' arrived at the stand.

"Hello I'm Pat, have you got any scrap you want to sell?" Chris was surprised, he thought his name was Mick? But quickly realised from his Irish accent that it was just one of those not terribly PC nicknames that antiques dealers had a habit of giving one another.

"Not really, there's some flatware over there but it's got to be a few pounds over scrap". Mick (Pat) quickly sifted through it all, hurriedly turning over each piece in his hands to check all the hallmarks and any crests, he was surprisingly nimble for such a big man, you'd expect to see him erecting a skyscraper with his bare hands, not sorting through Georgian and Victorian spoons.

"I'll have the lot" he said, putting it all into his seemingly bottomless leather bag "How much?"

Chris was delighted he'd never sold anything without somebody asking the price before, so he seized the opportunity and said fifty pounds more than he was going to ask and Pat duly paid him without a word of argument.

"I'll buy all and any scrap flatware you get, but you have to keep it ALL for me, don't sell anything before I've seen it, alright."

"Okay" replied Chris. Mick could have all the scrap flatware he ever got at that price!

Mick then reached into his waistcoat and drew out a small stack of papers, he took one and handed it to Chris.

"I'll pay a good premium if you find any of these."

The piece of A5 sized white paper had a Crest reproduced on it of a Lamb holding a staff or cross beneath a tree.
Below that it just had the words written:

"Old English Tablespoons marked JM, Exeter, 1792"

"Oh ok, right, I'll keep my eyes peeled" whilst folding the small piece of paper up and stuffing it into his wallet. He tried to engage Mick in a few pleasantries but as soon as he had arrived he'd gone again, it seemed Mick was just all business and no chat.

The morning then passed just as Vic had predicted it would. The sun was out and it got very busy with thick throngs of bustling people, jostling with one another simply to pass down the road and its side streets, wheatgrass juices and thai noodle salads in hand. Also as predicted Chris did indeed sell a number of small, uninspiring pieces (which had come in job lots) for quite spectacular prices to the unsuspecting American, Japanese, Russian and Chinese tourists.

"Good Day?" Vic returned, clearly in good humour himself and bearing teas and a bag of warm sausage rolls.

"Yeah, thanks, very good, though you could have told me that bloke's name was Pat not Mick!"

Vic laughed as he bit into a cheap sausage roll with half the pastry rolling down his shirt and jeans.

"What Mick? He don't mind. Did you get one? One of his bits of paper?"

Chris had clean forgotten with the bustle of the day and reached into his wallet where he'd put it.

Vic waved for him to put it away "I don't need to see it, none of us do, we've all got at least one. Hands them out to every silver dealer he sees, doubt there's one in the country that hasn't got one."

Chris was curious. "What is it his family silver or something?"

"Nah, hang on" stuffing the last of the sausage roll into his mouth Vic walked a few paces down to the street corner and whistled loudly, as everyone turned to look he shouted out "PETER! PETER!" then walked back to Chris.

"Peter can tell you, he's the mastermind when it comes to crests and shit like that." Chris discerned a palpable tone of disregard for academia in Vic's traders tones.

A minute later an older man than both Vic or Chris, with unkept grey curled hair, wearing a thick green stained woollen jumper (his trademark) joined them and was duly introduced by Vic.

"I was just telling Chris about Mick and his bits of paper, you looked it all up didn't you?" Vic then turned to Chris as if speaking privately, but as joke.

"He probably wanted to find out who it was for and cut out the middle man, eh Peter, was that it?"

Peter was a stern academic type and looked quite offended at the suggestion, "that's absolutely NOT the reason I did the research" he said firmly, though it absolutely was.

"No it came to nothing" Peter still rued the time he had wasted in finding out,

"The crest turned out to be for the Tempest family, of Stover House in Devon if remember rightly." He now continued as if giving a lecture to his eager students, "But they lost all their money in the late 1820's and sold up lock stock and barrel to Edward St Maur, the 11th Duke of Somerset when a railway venture bankrupted them. There are still some family relics in Torquay Museum, of the local building works they undertook and the like, worth a look if you're ever passing, quite interesting, but otherwise nothing, certainly no millionaire relatives buying tablespoons."

"Told you he'd know, a veritable encyclopedia our Peter" smiled Vic.

"Sausage roll Pete?" Vic pressed the now slightly cold dampened bag of sausage rolls next to Peters face as a thank you, he immediately recoiled in disgust and walked back to his stall. Vic shrugged his shoulders "Well, more for us" as he bit hungrily into to another sausage roll as he continued speaking, mouth half full.

"Yeah if you do find any of those spoons I reckon you can get a fortune off Mick. Dad sold him one once not knowing, big thick really heavy tablespoon it was. Mick fairly bit his hand off, Dad's still not got over letting it go so cheaply. Mind you I've only ever seen one other since then so the chances are slim."

"When was that?" asked Chris

"Bonhams, Knightsbridge about four, no five years ago. There was a little lot of spoons in for eighty quid, about what they were worth, but one of them was one of those tablespoons. I think the auctioneers must have told Mick as you never see him at the sales, but he turned up for this. Dad realised, he was still dealing back then, so decided to push him up on the price, especially as he'd sold him the other one so cheaply years before. When it got going Dad bid three, four, five hundred and Mick still kept bidding! Dad finally dropped out after pushing it up to eight hundred, getting scared he might buy it himself, but who knows when Mick would have stopped?"

All the time Vic had been talking Chris had been staring down, attentively this time, at the paper Mick had given him

"Oh hell!"

"What is it?"

"I only had one these spoons last month and bloody sold it!"

"Who too?"

"Oh a private buyer I've got for Exeter silver, a Doctor in Newbury. He's trying to get one piece from each year and this, 1792, was one of the years he was particularly missing, damn."

"Can't you buy it back?"

"I doubt it" sighed a deflated Chris, but there and then he thought he would at least give it a try.

A week later Chris was back at Portobello, though this time he wasn't a new face but a regular and the other dealers didn't quite crowd around his stand as he had hoped AND it had rained! The wheat grass drinking and thai salad eating wealthy tourists stayed away, footfall was down, though he reconciled himself with the thought he'd still got a fair bit of scrap for Mick.

When Mick turned up in his great coat, hobnail boots and gripping his eternal large leather bag, looking exactly a he had before Chris greeted him, though it barely elicited a response, beyond "got any scrap?"

Chris pulled out the pieces he'd been saving, again Mick darted through the crests and hallmarks as he'd done the previous week.

"I'm sorry I did have one of those spoons you were looking for a month or so ago, but I sold it. I did try get it back but I'm afraid the buyer isn't interested in selling" mentioned Chris as Mick was bent over looking, he straightened in an instant when he heard.

Mick looked up with a fixed stare that quite unsettled Chris for a moment. He paused and then said "How much do you want for this lot?"

Chris replied "What about five hundred the lot?" Though he knew there was only really just over four in scrap at the days bullion price.

'I'll give you eight hundred for it, eight hundred if you give me the contact for the collector with the spoon, I want to see if I can make him an offer myself."

Chris hesitated, it did feel wrong to do it, but what was the actual harm? Mick would only get the same response as he did and that would be an end to it, besides it had been a slow day and it was a full three hundred quid over the asking price.

"Done!"

The next morning Chris got an early call, it was Dr Melgrave, the collector of Exeter silver from Newbury, there had been a break-in overnight.

"I'm so sorry to hear that" said Chris and genuinely meant it when he thought what he'd done the day before. "Was much taken?"

"Luckily I disturbed the thief, though I didn't get a good look at him. All I could really tell in the dark was that he was big man. Hit me over the head then, as I fell to floor kicked me stoutly in the chest wearing a boot and ran off. It served to disturbed him enough though that he left almost all the valuable silver and thankfully just grabbed an odd handful of spoons. That's really why I was calling. Do you think you'd be free sometime next week to come round and write up a short valuation for the Insurers? What would you have to charge?"

Chris of course would charge nothing, it was the very least he could do under the circumstances and his terrible indiscretion, though he still couldn't be absolutely sure it had been Mick, there was a chance it might just be a coincidence but it was a small one.

The weeks passed without much further event, though Mick had no longer turned up at any of the fairs and markets he'd been a familiar face at for so many years. Such an imposing and unmistakable figure was quickly missed, especially by dealers who had been saving up boxes of scrap for him. Chris suspected he knew why.

It appeared in all the years, decades even, of people dealing with him no one had ever had a telephone number or address, certainly nothing like an email for Mick. He had just always been there, everywhere and then one day simply was not.

It was a few months later, Chris had almost forgotten the incident from his first couple of weeks at Portobello and was becoming a familiar face in the trade himself. He was down at a sale in Plymouth where several other silver dealers had turned up and, annoyingly for Chris, top amongst the topics of gossip and conversation was still what might have become of dear old Mick? It was a conversation Chris took pains to avoid, he still felt guilty about what he was now sure had happened.

Too many other, bigger dealers were there that day and Chris felt he had no chance of getting the lots he wanted, so after some negotiations he left with a few pounds in his pocket from being "persuaded" not to bid and thought he would do better by stopping off in Torquay and doing the shops and centres around there on the way back. The unwanted mention of Mick that day even put him in mind of Peters suggestion of months earlier to call in, perhaps briefly and look round the local Museum.

After a decent lunch but a fairly poor trawl of the local shops (he had only found two Georgian vinaigrettes and a set of thinly stamped Victorian wine labels for his troubles) Chris called into the Museum.

There were the familiar displays showing the history of the region, the odd Neolithic axe head and a smattering of large bronze (now green with corrosion) Roman coins dug up from the nearby site of Berry's Wood Hill Fort only a few miles down the road, a Bronze Age site which had been briefly occupied by the Romans. Of more interest was a display concerning the Templer family of the fabled set of spoons. This he eagerly read.

James Templer had been a local landowner and self made man. He had built the Stover Canal between 1790-1792 (which ran through the nearby town of Newton Abbot) to carry mined clay from the Bovey Basin to the port at Teignmouth. So fine and highly regarded was the Bovey clay that it was shipped all the way to Stoke from Teignmouth and the factories of the great potter Josiah Wedgwood.

Newton Abbot had also, it seemed, been a centre for the production of serge, renowned for it's cloth and great coats which were hard wearing and supplied to the military and any industrial or agricultural workers who could afford them, apparently a favourite for navvies working outdoors in the cold winter months. The one they had on display could have been mistaken for Mick's, though it was not so worn and tattered.

Besides that was a small display of locally made wares and a small showcase of Wedgwood pots made from the Bovey clay and then a small selection of silver items which really took Chris' attention.

There was a buckle, a pair of sugar tongs and a set of six teaspoons, all labelled as being by John Manley (III) of Newton Abbot, he worked in the town and had succeed in the business from his father but did have to send all of his silver to be assayed in Exeter. This was the same makers mark as the spoon he had sold with the Templer Crest. Is that why Mick had wanted them so much, because they were rare for being made in Newton Abbot, but to break into someone's house just for that? It seemed ridiculous.

An elderly part time assistant, who quite frankly hadn't had much else to do, had been watching Chris move throughout the ground floor of the Museum in the last hour or so and saw he was about to leave after paying particular attention to the display of locally made silver.

"You don't want to miss the best bit, Sir" the assistant called out.

Chris turned "I'm sorry?"

"The best bit, I saw you looking at the silver, well the best of it's just up the stairs. We had to put it there for security reasons, not easily accessible to the exits." The assistant pointed towards a short flight of stairs next to the lift. Chris certainly had five minutes spare to take a look.

At the top of the stairs was a brightly light, thick glass display case, clearly much, much sturdier than the ones downstairs, he was glad he had bothered to come up.

Inside was a large rectangular silver tray about 15 inches long and 10 inches wide , but it had been broken in two pieces and there was still a large third piece missing. Still what there was, was certainly worth seeing. It had a beaded edge enclosing a chased border of fruiting vines and ram's masks. The central scene was of a open temple with trees behind and a small brazier wreathed in flame with a figure of Goddess (?) all in Roman dress but with beautifully chased open wings and holding a upright dagger in one hand, the rest of the scene was sadly incomplete.

Chris walked around to see the back of the tray which was by contrast to the delicate work on the front entirely plain except for six riveted chamfered brackets tightly holding the two broken pieces together. It had been inscribed by whoever had done the work.

"Found in the grounds of the Canal Works near St Peter and St. Paul, Newton Abbot, by Workmen, 3rd July 1792.

Presented to Mr James Templer who paid for its restoration.

J.M Fecit 1792"

His clear interest in the tray had caused one of the passing curators to stop and engage Chris.

"Lovely isn't it, our Lanx, but sadly incomplete."

"Lanx?" replied Chris, who had not paused to read the extensive label next to the case.

"Yes it's a Roman form of tray, some people think it was used for serving food and drink at banquets, other maintain it was for sacrificial offerings."

"What's the decoration?" asked Chris

"Oh it the figure of Invidia, well you'll know here better as Nemesis winged balancer, dark faced goddess, daughter of justice' as Mesomedes wrote."

Helen the curator could see Chris looked slightly puzzled at her reply,

"Well put it like this, you wouldn't want to get on the wrong side of her" she smiled.

"Shame it's incomplete, what happened to the other piece, didn't they discover it?"

"No, I'm sad to say the three workmen, all navvies employed by James Templer to dig out a lock on the Canal found it whole. There is evidence that they simply chopped into three roughly equal pieces with blows from something like their spades. It is after all quite heavy and solid, almost pure, silver, yes it would have been its value in bullion that interested them at that time, never its historic merit."

"You mean it's scrap price?" replied Chris.

"Well yes, I suppose you could put it like that. Indeed that's probably what happened to the missing piece. A colleague made a study of it before we got the funding for the new display case, took it and weighed what we have here and allowing for the repairs it weighs just about 75 ounces. Given its slightly over a third that's missing it could have been 35 perhaps 40 ounces of silver that the third man got away with."

"Third man?"

"Yes the account at the time, you see here." Helen pointed to the extensive labels around the case which Chris had failed to read, "...of the three men who found it, two had a change of heart the next day and surrendered their pieces to the landowner and were rewarded for their honesty, the third by then had already absconded with his ill gotten gains."

"and it's never turned up?"

"Well, it was probably sold and melted down, if it was 35-40 ounces you could turn it into a lot of things, a large tankard or perhaps a couple of mugs, a pair of candlesticks..."

"or a set of spoons, a set of twelve tablespoons!" interrupted Chris, Helen looked at him with slight surprise,

"Well, yes, you'd probably have to make them fairly large and heavy but I suppose, how odd though, how very odd, you should say that about spoons."

She briefly trailed off in thought, then resumed.

"I'd never though of it before but we had a man donate such a set of spoons only a few months ago to the Museum. Odd chap, a large man a broad accent, perhaps Scottish, I can't quite remember though he did have terribly noisy hobnail boots. He insisted we could only have the spoons if they were displayed alongside the Lanx. We refused of course, we couldn't afford them the same importance but they were of local interest so we compromised and said we would add them to the display on the lower floor. He seemed content with that."

"I didn't see them downstairs?" queried a now agitated but

increasingly curious Chris.

Helen replied, "Well we would have them on display now but after he handed them to me I went to fetch a deed of gift form. I was only gone and minute of two but when I got back he'd simply gone. Not that any of the staff saw him leave. No name or forwarding address, nothing, so we're still waiting to complete the due diligence on them prior to putting them on public display. They're only in storage in my office, if you're really interested, well would you like to see them?"

Chris nodded slowly and followed Helen just a few steps into her office. She sat at her desk and gestured for him to sit down in the chair opposite, she swivelled round to the large safe behind her and unlocked it with a key from around the bunch attached to her belt, taking out a small tray from one of the steel shelves upon which was a parcel of spoons wrapped in white crinkled acid free tissue paper. She unwrapped them one at a time and laid them down in front of Chris in a row.

"You have a look at these, whilst I just go and fetch something to test your theory."

Chris picked up one of the twelve thick heavy silver tablespoons, he turned it over to see the marks of John Manley III of Newton Abbot assayed in Exeter in 1792, it was all very familiar.

As he turned it back around to look at the crest Helen returned from the other side of the office with a set of digital scales. She took the spoons and the one Chris was holding.

"Let's see if you're right."

As the last spoon was placed onto the balances they displayed a digital readout of 36.10, just over three ounces each.

"Near enough, so it could have been twelve spoons." smiled Helen, oblivious of any connection. "Sadly we'll never really know, but at least this a lovely set and by the same man who repaired the Lanx, we were thrilled to get them, though I haven't traced the crest yet." She pointed to the engraving at the top of the stem, it was of a lamb holding a staff seated beneath an Oak tree.

"It's James Templer's crest" said a slightly pale Chris, as he let the chair he was sitting on take the fullest weight of his body.

"Are you sure?" replied a surprised Helen at the seemingly effortless and speedy identification of the crest.

"Positive" said Chris "Absolutely positive"

The Hinoki Box

Jan had always loved Japanese Art since he was a boy, it had
been his father's business at the turn of the century and he had
joined it as a young man just after the Second World War.
Back then you could buy Japanese works of art for a pittance
because of their post war associations, with an abundance of
material flooding onto the market. Now, after a lifetime's
dealing his two grandsons Walter and Dirk were following him
into the business, taking over the reigns in quite different
times.

Jan was almost in his nineties, just the well worn figure head
for the business, someone for his grandsons to occasionally
dust off and present to their clients in the name of continuity,
that one thing any up and coming new dealer simply couldn't
offer. The simple "Est.1895" on their letter heads and invoices
was worth its weight in gold. This was why Jan had been flown
half way round the world by Dirk. Fine Art Asia was only a
few days away and they had taken a considerably large stand.
Jan had agreed to the trip as long as they could leave early and
stop off at the Tokyo National Museum, an old favourite of his
as possibly this would be the last time he was able to visit.

Jan had sat in the pin drop quiet of one of the Museum's
galleries, admiring a selection of fine Kakiemon porcelain in
the display case in front of him. Moments later, to much
embarrassment, his phone went off in his pocket, loudly
playing the tune from Van Der Valk that his great grandson
had thought to put as the ringtone as a joke before he'd left.

He hurried as fast as any fit but startled man of his age could to lift the slim smooth and now increasingly slippery metal case out of his deep coat pocket, the folds of material seemingly unwilling to set it free and bring silence back to the Honkan (Japanese Gallery).

"Hello, hello, who is it?"

Jan was more than a little peeved his contemplation of the fine case of Japanese ceramics had been interrupted, but still spoke in a hushed tone out of respect for his surroundings, no one of any sensitivity shouted in a Museum.

"Grandad, it's Walter. Sorry to call but I think Dirk's gone and done it again."

"What now?" replied the old man with the tone of resignation that told he had been mediating the two men's disputes and petty arguments since they were little boys.

"I've just had John, Lord Walmsey, in the shop, he'd come up to London specially to see that Muromachi Period Negoro bowl. I went into the stock room to get it and it's nowhere to be found. Either we've been broken into by a Negoro Bowl fetishist or my bloody brother has whipped it off to the fair without telling me…(there was then a very tense pause)…AGAIN!"

"Look it's done now Walter, don't upset yourself, just leave me to deal with it."

If Jan had had a good and successful life as a dealer the only thing he now worried about was the future for his grandsons when he left them behind. Dirk had the flair and salesmanship of a good dealer but was always too eager to put his own immediate needs first. Walter was a superb academic but that had made him bookish and slightly awkward with good wealthy clients who weren't fanatical collectors. He really needed to reign in Dirks excesses and see that the two of them worked together. Being in the Museum after all these years, the first time Dirk had come with him, gave him an excellent idea of how to make his point.

Just as Jan had put his phone back in his pocket Dirk walked back into the Gallery that his grandfather was in. Looking at the old man perched inches away from a display case on the small collapsible shooting stick that had become his constant companion.

"Ok Gramps? Ready to go?"

"Patience Dirk, patience, we've got all day. I just had your brother on the phone from London, something about a missing Negoro ware bowl?"

Dirk shrugged his shoulders,

"I had a client, a good client that wanted to know if we still had it and I said yes, what's wrong with that?"

"What's wrong is that it was being held for John Walmsley to look at."

"Yeah, but you know he only ever buys a few things and the client that asked was Mr Tsui, you know how important he is to us."

Jan gave his grandson a good steady look for a moment and lowered his tone, though it was still an affectionate one,

"Look, you can't always do everything and please everyone, sometimes the best thing to say is 'no'. I know we don't like to but we can get ourselves in more trouble by not refusing the impossible."

"That might be how things were done in your day, but the world's changed."

The old man looked a little disheartened at his grandson's reply, so he determined to try drive his point in the most compelling way he knew possible.

"Have I ever told you about the Cypress (Hinoki) writing box?"

"No, I can't recall you ever mentioning it, what is it?"

"It' a piece here in the Museum, I first saw it about forty years ago now."

Jan got up by shifting half his body weight on the shooting stick handle and briefly leaning over then straightened himself to the cracking sound of two or three stiff joints,

"Just wait there" he instructed Dirk, pointing with a governly finger at the floor and then walked off to a nearby gallery assistant.

After a few words were exchanged the assistant radioed through to the curatorial department and five minutes later a small bald desiccated Japanese man, slightly bent over by the passage of time, though still spry, nimbly walked into the gallery smiling broadly at Jan. The men embraced as friends who had known each other for at least half their lifetimes.

"Aki, so good to see you"

"Jan it is such a great honour and a pleasure to see you here again"

The two men had worked together in Jan's early days in organising a small loan exhibition held at his London gallery in 1973 of the Art of the Netsuke (small carved toggles) from the Edo period. The slim catalogue of the Exhibition is still somewhat sought after. Since then they had been firm friends and on the occasion when the Museum wished to make a purchase in Europe they would always ask Jan to represent them. He had visited many times but it had been over ten years since his last trip.

"Aki, this is my youngest grandson Dirk, you've heard me speak of him often, I wondered if it would be possible to see the Hinoki writing box?"

Aki seemed a little hesitant at first and asked, "It's in the stores now, does he know the story?"

Jan shook his head, "I think it would be helpful if he did."

Aki asked them to follow them to his office. It would take him about twenty minutes to fetch the box out from storage and they were welcome to sit and have tea. Jan thanked him and said it would be ideal, in the meantime he would tell Dirk the tale.

"What's all this about a simple wooden writing box?" Dirk whispered in a low voice to his Grandfather once Aki had gone to leave.

Jan replied, "I'll tell you this story just as it was told to me when I met the former curator of the collections in the late 70's. The box had been given to the collection by the great grandson of the man who had made, Kyuzo Toyo."

Toyo had been from a family of artists that had worked in lacquer, true Japanese lacquer (Urushi), which is the annually harvested sap of the Rhus Vernicifera.

After much processing it can be used to make exquisite objects of almost any form imaginable. Toyo had developed a great skill within his father's and grandfather's workshop and had even been sent to work as an apprentice under Kyuzo VI when he was appointed court lacquerer to the Shogun Ienari at the beginning of the nineteenth century. After seven years Toyo returned to his small rural home some fifty miles from the capital (Edo) to take over his families workshop. He had not cared for the hustle and bustle of city life.

Toyo quickly established a reputation for excellence in the province, and whilst some of the wealthier merchants still sought to commission the artists in the capital, Toyo became a favourite of the local officials and scholars and having the distinction of making pieces for the local Daimyo (Lord).

His style was more traditional, more subtle with his love of the local countryside and nature as his subject matter. In the capital the fashion was of the Ukiyo-e with its courtesans and theatres, it was a far showier style of work epitomised by the taste for

Shibayama inlays, bold and bright with elaborate subjects and forms, quite at odds with Toyo's style.

Toyo's workshop was up in the hills and he had a number of apprentices under him, all performing their given tasks to the very best of their abilities, always under Toyo's watchful and sharp eye, his meticulous attention to detail was legendary.

It was the spring of 1853 and the Daimyo had sent a messenger to the workshop asking that Toyo attend him. Duly he set off, having first given instructions to his assistants that no important work should be carried out in the few days he would be absent.

Upon arriving to the Daimyo's home he was given an audience where the Lord told him that he had given Toyo the honour of fashioning a lacquer Suzuribako (writing box) for presentation to the newly invested ruler Tokugawa Iesada, but it would need to be ready by the end of the year, a little over six months.

The honour was as great as the responsibility. This would be the greatest undertaking of Toyo's long career and everything he knew had to be perfect.

Six months may seem a long time, but in the preparation of a lacquer object it was painfully short. First a carcass in wood, paper or leather had to be taken and the Urishi (lacquer) which had been graded and sorted carefully painted on in layers, then dried and polished down before the next one could be applied. A fine piece may have up to a hundred layers of lacquer applied to it before it was finished.

Toyo did not waste any time. He had decided to decorate a simple rectangular box with layers of gold and black lacquer in a style known as sumi-e togidashi. It was a very subtle and refined technique where the lacquer would almost imitate an ink painting, and the subject he decided would be the Cherry trees around his own workshop, their ornate twisting branches, subtle blossoms and leaves.

"Go to the store and fetch out the best large pieces of Hinoki (Cypress) timber for the carcass"

Toyo instructed his box maker Kenzo as soon as he'd returned to his workshop.

The nature of the work meant that timbers had to be seasoned for years to ensure that they would not warp or twist being the thin core to the objects that were made. Smaller pieces such as Inro might be made of Sakura (Cherry wood) or even thick paper and leather, but larger Bako (boxes) needed a stronger wooden core and the very choicest timber to use was Cypress wood.

Kenzo returned moments later "Master Toyo we do not have any seasoned Cypress in large enough pieces, only Pine and Cherry."

The choice, or rather the compromise, would have been to join two pieces of the Cypress wood he had together or use single pieces of the slightly inferior but perfectly usable timber. Possibly Toyo may have done this were the client a merchant and it not an important piece, but as it was for the Daimyo to give to the Tokugawa ruler he simply could not compromise, his pride over his work and quest for perfection got in the way. Nor could he delay.

"Go at once to Yenso the master carpenter and ask for two broad pieces of his best seasoned Hinoki, he must have some."

Yenso was a Master carpenter only a village away and would be sure to have the well seasoned timber that Toyo's box maker Kenzo required to pare down to form the delicate carcass of the Writing box.

Kenzo returned that evening but without the cypress wood. He explained to his master that Yenso the carpenter did have some broad pieces of cypress that had been aged for four years, perfect for the box, but it had all been bought by the widow of a local farmer a month earlier, to build a small shrine to her late husband, honouring the God Raiden (Thunder and Rain) for the lifetime of temperate weather and good harvests that the farmer and his wife had enjoyed.

Toyo could not believe that two short lengths of broad timber could not be spared for him to make a box for the Imperial court and was enraged that it would be used for a peasant's shrine. He immediately set off to talk to Yenso himself and was going to return with the cypress wood under any circumstances.

A day later Toyo had indeed implored and demanded the sections of timber that he required be given to him by Yenso. He told him that this was for the Daimyo and the Court and that the carpenter would simply have to substitute another wood in parts of the shrine that would not be seen, or would be covered by decoration. Yenso, though he felt in his heart it was wrong, was unable to refuse Toyo's emphatic demands.

Once Toyo had returned with the long section of broad

seasoned Cypress wood work began in earnest and with great speed upon the Suzuribako.

Kenzo took the timber and, with broad razor sharp blades began to smooth the surface of the wood and pare it down into thin and light sections which would form the rectangular boxes cover, sides and base. Each piece was cut and planed at precise angles and fitted together like a glove, the only spacing between the parts allowing for the width of the finished layers of lacquer.

Then two assistants took turns in applying the nurimono-shi, or base layers of lacquer over the core. The lacquer itself would only properly harden in high humidity and warm temperatures over 27 degrees Celsius. Water ran down the walls of the drying room and the temperature was oppressive. As each layer dried and hardened it would be polished mirror smooth with a mixture of burnt clay and powdered deer's horn.

Several months passed in the preparation of the base layers of the box, with Toyo inspecting the progress at every stage, making sure every surface was even and as smooth as the surface of a still pond.

It was then time for the decoration to begin. Toyo had before him gold and silver powders, graded and sorted into small bamboo dusting tubes (tsutsu) with various sizes of gauze across the tops. He could sprinkle fine gold onto the wet lacquer for an even matt finish, or sprinkle various sizes of gold or silver flakes to give different effects of ground, even placing larger pieces by hand with the tip of a needle to create an irregular patchwork of tiny gold stones, the Gyobu-Nashiji technique he had learnt years earlier, a favourite of the Kajikawa family of lacquer Artists.

He decided that all the edges of the box would be simply matt gold (fundame) but the interior surfaces would be a fine nashiji ground built up and polished down so it would subtly sparkle through the final layers of clear lacquer, above that he would paint fine raised scattered cherry leaves with his neji-fude (rat's hair brushes).

The cover he had already decided to decorate in the sumi-e togidshai technique. He would build up a dense rich gold ground and then finely raise the decoration of the Cherry trees in black lacquer. Once finished it would be covered in layer after layer of the gold lacquer until nothing could be seen and then polished down by his own hand with a mixture of powdered deer horn as an abrasive, until flush and smooth, revealing the black lacquer decoration of the Cherry trees through the gold ground. The whole effect would not be unlike a scholarly ink painting, highly favoured at court, but the box itself would have a hard and mirror like surface.

The work continued day and night. Toyo barely slept and stayed in his workshop to complete the box in time for the Daimyo to present it in the Edo court. His only disturbance would be the farmer's widow who had found out from the honest Yenso that a piece of her Hinoki wood for the small peasant's shrine had been taken by Toyo.

She regularly cried and lamented at the foot of the workshop only for Toyo to get his apprentices to shoo her away, he could not countenance interruptions to his work, this was to be his most important piece.

The six months had flown by faster than a river about to break its banks, it was now only three days before the Daimyo would pass by on his way to Edo to collect the writing box.

Toyo was nearly finished, he had gotten Kenzo to make a presentation box for the Suzuribako, lining it with the finest silk brocade. The accompanying brush, in carved layered lacquer had been finished and the water dropper which Toyo decided should be made in Shakudo and Shibuichi (alloys of gold and silver) in the form of a Cherry blossom had been delivered from the workshop of the nearby goldsmith and carefully fitted. All that was left was the final polishing down of the cover of the box to reveal the Cherry trees he had built up in black lacquer below.

Jan had to stop his story there, it had been near enough twenty minutes and Aki had returned for the stores with a plain cherry wood box, painted on the front in Japanese characters was an inscription:

"A box made by my late master Kyuzo Toyo and another. Finished by my hand, Kenzo, 1853"

Dirk looked up at Aki, the story had fascinated him and he wanted to see the box, the fine work work of a master lacquerer which had taken so much time.

Aki motioned to him that he could take the cover from the pine outer case and look at the writing box within, he lifted it and suddenly his face was overwhelmed with a taught look of shock and surprise at the scene that greeted him below, as it had Toyo, over a hundred and fifty years ago, when had begun, finally to polish down and remove the surface layers of gold to reveal the fine painted decoration below.

Toyo had not found the cherry blossom boughs swaying in a gentle breeze that he had meticulously built up in layers of black lacquer.

Instead he saw a bearded figure, almost dancing, surrounded by a circle of drums and clouds, his face twisted in rage and anger.

As Toyo polished the surface down further he revealed the scene of a figure seated in a workshop, familiar, similar to his own?

The man was only visible from behind but was bent forward over a work table as he himself now was, in polishing the box down. A chill ran through the master at his work as he continued smoothing the surface down of this now unfamiliar writing box, revealing dark even lines of pelting rain and delicate silvered bolts issuing from the dancing heavenly figure above. A shutter in the workshop suddenly blew open and slammed shut, he heard the hard pelting of heavy rain upon the wooden roof falling like a hundred nails tipped from a great box, then an all too brief moment of dead silence before a great, shattering roar of thunder, louder than any he heard before shouting out of the dark night sky.

"It's the God Raiden" pointed out Aki to Dirk,

"here in the top corner of the box and below, below is quite rare indeed, a depiction of a late Edo period workshop with an artist at his finishing table."

Jan and Aki then exchanged a knowing silent glance to one another as the young man sat stunned and open mouthed.

Dirk turned to his Grandfather, "What became of Toyo?"

"The best I could find out was that he died a day or so before the box was finished, struck down in a fierce storm. His pupil Kenzo did the little work needed to put all the parts of the writing box together and did the final polishing, though not to much end as when presented with it, the Daimyo chose not it to give it to Tokugawa Iesada after all, it was felt to be a bad omen, unlucky."

The old man paused,

"Toyo had favoured his own needs over those of all others, which with hindsight, seemed a most unwise thing to do."

All three men sat quietly as they thought they just heard a distant roar of thunder despite the bright Sun shining through the office's windows. It made them all uneasy and it urged Aki to move swiftly to replace the simple pine cover over the lacquer Suzuribako, decorated as it was with a Thunder God who, for a moment almost, appeared to be grinning.

Shards

"You couldn't give me a lift to the station this morning on your way to school could you love?"

Bethan heard Harry's voice clearly from their bedroom upstairs along with the intermittent clomping sound of his feet hitting the bare oak boards they'd stripped back and spent three days polishing together last summer. He was trying to get dressed as she was finishing off breakfast in the kitchen.

"I was going in early anyway. We've got a meeting with the Head about young Davy again so I can drop you off in about.."

Bethan paused and hurriedly turned to look at the wristwatch on her left hand as she deftly shoved half a buttered slice of toast, dripping with best marmalade, into Harry's smiling mouth with the other,

"..ten minutes, is that ok?"

"Yes that's great" Harry managed to say with golden crumbs of toast and a vivid drop of crystal orange spilling across his chin. He wiped it clean with the sleeve of his freshly ironed shirt.

"Christ! Don't do that you messy bugger" Bethan picked up a nearby, nearly clean tea towel and ran it under the cold tap, pulling Harry's sleeve towards her and rubbing it briskly to remove any offending trace of breakfast. She was used to dealing with the messy and unruly boys in her class, Harry was often no different, just bigger.

"Right, I'll just get my stuff and we'll go"

Harry went to the battered oak Georgian bureau in the living room. It was about the first piece of furniture they had bought together for the new house, not because they particularly liked it but it was at one of the auctions Harry was buying at and going for ten quid. How could Bethan not resist putting her hand up in the air to buy it for ten quid? The handles were wrong, Victorian brass bail handles and the fall front had shrunk in at the sides where it had been cleated together so there were two parallel faint cracks, but for a tenner, plus the slap (saleroom commission) and a borrow of Dave's van to get it had become the nerve centre of their home.

Harry pulled open a few of the small rectangular drawers, mostly stuffed with old bills, receipts, pens and the odd paper clip.

"Where's the miniature?" he called out to the kitchen.

"Secret drawer" came Bethan's reply. Ahh yes remembered Harry as he pulled out one of the columns beside the central compartment of the interior of the bureau which was actually a secret drawer. He tipped it up and a small velvet bag slipped into his hands secured with a draw string. He opened it up to see the oval gold frame of a fine portrait miniature of a young boy (he had wished it was a young girl, they were always more saleable) painted in the manner of Andrew Plimmer, though it was unsigned. He slipped it back into the bag and placed it gently in the inside pocket of his coat, turning to see Bethan already at the front door holding the car keys and her bag.

"You ready?"

Harry briefly tapped both trouser pockets to check for wallet and phone and nodded yes as they both left the house and got into the little red Golf parked just outside.

"I should be back about five, depending how the trains are running out of London. I've only got to run into Oliver's gallery, drop this off and if I've got time go and see clearance Fred on the way back to the station. I'll give you a call if I'm going to be late."

Bethan pulled up to the small local station and Harry jumped out, giving her a kiss on the cheek, but slightly missing and catching her ear as he could see the train wasn't far off arriving.

"Bye, see you tonight!"

The train was a hit and miss affair, sometimes the commuters would be on a slightly later one, but not today. It was jammed and he managed just to get a small bit of floor to himself between the already packed carriages, though it was unfortunately near to the toilets and a man with a fold up bicycle who was oblivious to any injury it's sharp edges may inflict on the unsuspecting passengers who were at such close quarters. Harry quietly slipped his hand into his jacket and cradled the small velvet bag to protect the miniature inside from any accidental destructive blows, he kept it there, safe for the entire journey of the 7.12 to Euston.

Getting into the station and off the battery farm carriages was a relief, he strode down the station platform and through the barrier to the tube, pausing only to buy one of those cheap hot croissants with a limp, steamed wet slice of bacon and cheese forced into it. Harry barely noticed how unpleasantly chewy it was as he wolfed it down.

He'd navigated his way to Bond St station after half an hour on the tube and was glad to be in the not so fresh air of Bond St, walking down South Molton Street, past Grays and then on to Oliver's Gallery in Maddox Street.

The small, almost Lilliputian black railings ran around the front of the shop and set off the white Portland stone Ionic columns that flanked the tinted glass door, making them seem enormous. "Oliver Culver and Associates" was finely written in gilt letters on the door, Harry rang the bell and a buzzer sounded to admit him egress.

"Morning Oliver."

"Morning my dear boy, lovely to see you"

A very slim elegantly dressed man, slightly greying, in his late 50's wearing the Art World shibboleth of red trousers terminating in a pair of Lobb shoes ushered Harry with several waves of his hand towards a good thick leather Barcelona chair in the middle of the gallery. Knowing Oliver Harry suspected it was entirely possible that it was one of Miles van der Rohe's originals.

"Let's see it then." Oliver purred as he sat opposite Harry.

The velvet bag appeared from his pocket and the draw string loosened to reveal the miniature within. Oliver immediately picked it up and brought it close to his eye, turning it lightly back and forth in the light coming from the large front window, bringing up every detail of the brushwork into clear focus.

"It is delightful." he exclaimed, but then as quickly placed it back on the table and continued in a more disparaging tone.

"Such a shame it's a boy not a girl"

Harry tried not to let out a small chuckle given Oliver's predatory reputation in the trade, when again, he wondered would those words ever issue from his lips?

"But it's a Plimmer and a nice one, I did email you all the images last week Oliver"

"Yes, it's nice, but it's only an attribution, it's not signed is it? I haven't missed a signature?"

Harry knew Oliver had been told it was unsigned when they agreed a price over the phone last week. Then, before it had entered his gallery, he had been all too eager to acquire it. It was one of the oldest but still most effective ploys, though Harry was having none of it, not after the train journey and croissant he'd just had to endure.

"Most of them aren't signed and you know it Oliver, it's yes or no to what we agreed or I'll take it to Laurie, he wanted a look at it anyway"

Oliver could see the bluff hadn't worked and his tone immediately changed to an ameliorated one.

"No, of course it's lovely and by Plimmer, his hand is unmistakable, now how much did we say, three?"

"and a half" quickly added Harry.

"Yes, three and a half, cash as always I suppose?" Oliver answered his own question as he rose and approached his left hand side desk draw, opening it up and taking out the envelope with three and a half thousand pounds in it to give to Harry. It was next to another envelope with three thousand pounds and another with two, but the old ploy hadn't worked and today Oliver wasn't going to get quite the bargain he had hoped.

The awful awkward business of business out of the way both men relaxed, Harry with cash, most of it a tidy profit in his pocket and Oliver with a miniature he had already sold to a client in California, sight unseen, for fifteen thousand.

"So what are you doing today, going to view Christie's? Nice sale I'm told an estate from your neck of the woods, well just outside Bristol, I'll be viewing it myself this afternoon."

"Have a few calls to make after you and then shall probably head back before the commuter rush back, might pop into the V&A if I've got time."

"Ah yes, education! The main stay of our business, the great and hallowed halls of THE museum" Oliver turned and briefly looked out of the window at the shops of his rival specialists and continued in a caustic tone of lamentation

"Not that you're likely to see any of this lot there, it's just not like it used to be."

Harry took that as his cue to leave and got up shaking Oliver's hand and telling him he'd let him know the next time something good turned up in one of the out of the way sales in his neck of the woods.

As Harry walked back to the tube station, back up South Molton Street he could feel the warmth of the three and a half grand burning a hole in his pocket, he was dangerously near to Gray's Antiques market and he knew clearance Fred would be there.

Frederick Purnell Works of Art had a small six foot stand and actually spent most of his time with his two sons doing house clearances along the south coast. He'd cleared so many deceased estates in his lifetime that the other dealers said he should be driving a hearse not a van but it had been the source of many an interesting find. So much so that Fred had, early on, picked out the best pieces and taken them to London to sell, cutting out three or four middlemen making their own turn on every piece, though with the Internet these days so much had changed. Harry had been buying odds and ends from Fred for years, he always had something new to show him.

"Morning Fred, cuppa?" Harry had stopped for a couple of teas and taken one into Fred, white two sugars.

"Blimey what are you doing up here at this time of the morning?" Harry didn't like to say who he'd been calling on (contacts are contacts) so slipped into the standard reply

"I've come all the way up here because I know you've got the best stuff Fred, so come on what have you been hiding?"

Fred took out a small Victorian leather jewellery box and placed it on the glass display counter in front of him.

"Just odds and ends, a nice bit of costume from a flat in Hove last Saturday, rest was firewood except for a nice early landscape but that went straight away"

The old man tipped the open jewellery box up as the contents spilled out in front of Harry.

"Any of it gold?" Harry knew Fred would have tested every unmarked chain and pendant in the box before bringing it out.

"Nah, but some nice costume."

Fred pointed out a heart shaped pendant inset with black dot paste and set in silver which was late George III and a small blue and white enamel ring, neither excited Harry as much as the triple row of quite, quite horrible 1930's cultured pearls mixed in with them.

"Shame these aren't real" Harry picked them up to show Fred, making sure the clasp which secured them was closed tightly in his palm,

"Yeah, I could retire if they were."

"So how much? Might just buy them for Bethan as a souvenir if they don't cost the earth."

Fred paused and looked at the three strands of pearls, some with the glossy paper thin layer of nacre peeling off them.

"Well, the trendy types still love them so it's got to be one fifty."

Harry did his best to look shocked and conceal his delight, "what about one and a quarter, cash?"

Fred nodded as he thought Harry might only be pushed up to a hundred.

Harry stuffed the pearls into his pocket and paid Fred, wishing him all the best and hurried out to the street. After he was safely a good few steps away he paused at a bin and pulled the pearls out of his pocket. He broke the strings off letting them all cascade into the bin, taking care not to damage or lose the clasp that was securing them. It was an oval disc of white gilt metal inset on one side with a small portrait miniature, of a young woman in early Georgian dress. It was very fine and almost certainly by Gervase Spencer.

Harry went to head straight back to Oliver's Gallery but then it occurred to him that he'd probably already gone out. He knew he'd be at Christie's in the afternoon. He'd grab an early lunch and head off to King St, even though there was a slight chance he might bump into Claire there.

After popping into the pub for a small bowl of chips and a pint, he was after all not driving anywhere today, Harry walked the few short steps down to King Street where a row of Christie's red flags billowing in the light breeze above him seemed to guide him towards the steps leading up to the impressive stone faced portico of one of the country's oldest Auction Houses, hallowed ground. A uniformed figure obscured through smoke tinted glass opened the doors as he approached and entered through to the warm, thickly carpeted and hushed cathedral like atmosphere. The bustling and noisy street outside silenced as the heavy doors behind him fell shut with the bespoke ease of a Bentley car door. Harry approached reception and asked, quietly, where the sale was on view, he was pointed to the series of galleries immediately to his right.

It seemed he was the only person viewing, though it was a Monday afternoon and the sale wasn't until the end of the week. One or two quiet figures were dotted around the room in silent contemplation of their catalogues. He hadn't bought one as they were thirty five pounds each, besides he was really only looking for Oliver, the prospective purchaser, though he did not know it, of the Gervase Spencer clasp Harry had nestling in his pocket.

He continued looking through the galleries, there were lots of examples of high Victorian and Aesthetic movement pieces of furniture, Bevan, Godwin et al. Not Harry's taste but all lovely examples but all with lovely estimates too. Nothing started at less than twenty thousand and went up, fifty, a hundred from there, all well out of his league.

As he continued through the galleries he passed one of the star lots of the sale, an unrecorded painting of a Mythological figure, thought to be the Greek goddess Nike (wings not trainers) by Waterhouse, thin and sparsely clothed beside a shallow pool within a temple with painted walls, it was, according to the label commissioned by the estate's owner Richard Cornwallis in around 1897 and had a whopping estimate of one to one and a half million, though his painting of The Siren had made nearly four only last year, but in that the mythological figure had been completely nude, which always made a difference in the very discerning Art Market.

The last of the three rooms displaying the lots from Acton Hall comprised some fine 19th century ceramics, mostly

Worcester and Wedgwood copies in the classical style, each exhibition quality and again with notes showing they had been specifically commissioned by Cornwallis. Opposite those were a selection of large, striking Etruscan terracotta vases, all restored but with unusual scenes of a procession of infants to a temple, soothsayers or priests worshipping at a shrine and another with deities with hammers and wings, their arms entwined with serpents, one a vivid blue. In front of them was a small flat case containing some fine intaglio carved hardstones and gilt bronze zoomorphic mounts and spear heads, it struck Harry as a very odd collection of items, but he took great interest in the carved hardstones, it might be the sort of thing he'd find one day in a Victorian setting being sold as nineteenth century.

Just as he'd about finished viewing, with Oliver still nowhere to be seen he heard a soft familiar voice behind him.

"Harry, is that you? Long time no see."

He turned to see Claire, immaculate in a tailored jacket and skirt, her long blonde hair kept up from her face by an alice band. They had both studied Fine Art at Southampton and whilst he had been the rising star, he'd dropped out to start dealing full time, whereas she'd gone on to get her degree and with her family connections in the very best circles secured a foot in the door at Sotheby's, he'd read in the trade paper she'd been head hunted by Christie's valuations department only a couple of years earlier, though his abiding memory of her was half wrapped up in a blanket outside the student halls of residence at one o'clock in the morning as some drunken idiot had pulled the fire alarm. Things might have worked out very differently were it not for the random fateful interruption for them both.

"Claire, lovely to see you" They both lightly embraced for a moment and exchanged a barely touching, though nonetheless awkward, kiss.

"You viewing today? Anything in particular. I can give you some extra background if you like, it was my job and I had to go out and clear the Hall a couple of months ago."

"I like the Waterhouse" Harry joked,

"It's just a little beyond my pocket"

He went to pull out the empty lining of his trouser pocket to make the point forgetting he'd got over three grand stuffed in there, hurriedly and embarrassingly pushing it back in as the notes spilled out.

"Well, you're clearly doing something right" exclaimed Claire. No one really ever saw cash these days, certainly not at Christie's.

"Look come up to my office and we can catch up over a cup of tea."

Harry, having quickly scanned the gallery for sight of Oliver whilst Claire was speaking, sadly to no avail, nodded and followed her up to the valuations department on the second floor.

It was a crammed office with three desks bordered on all sides with bookcases groaning with old sale catalogues, files and reference works. Claire's desk was small and in the corner, covered with catalogue proofs, post it reminders and a huge old pot full of pens of every description. She cleared a stack of files off the chair next to hers and Harry sat down.

"Well it's cosy" Harry said as Claire leaned forward to tidy up the paperwork strewn desk as best she could.

"Tea okay? White with one isn't it?"

"Great memory, yes that will be lovely."

Harry lent forward and picked up a stack of old Victorian studio card photo's form Claire's desk.

"That's him" she pointed to the photographs in Harry's hand as she stood waiting for the now grumbling and hissing electric kettle to boil. Stretching out her arm to pick up the sorry broken fruitwood tea caddy which had been unsold and unclaimed for more years than anyone could remember, its new role being the communal tea bag holder for the whole department.

"That's Richard Cornwallis. We were lucky to find those still amongst his papers at the Hall. Two or three of them are reproduced in the catalogue as they show him with a lot of the items, particularly the Antiquities which gives us a lovely cast iron provenance for the whole collection."

"Have you got a spare catalogue Claire?" Harry wasn't going to let the chance of a free one slip by without trying.

"Here" she handed him one from a stack of them in an open box on the floor,

"You'll see the images on pages 3-6, I had to research and write the introduction myself"

"Lovely job" complimented Harry. "What's this image here? He looks much younger and is he abroad somewhere?"

"That was taken when he was about 19 the best I can find out. He'd been from a local middle class family, his father was a Vicar and when he died Richard took a small inheritance and toured Greece and Italy. It was whilst out there for two or three years that he undertook some excavations at Tarquinia, that's where we think all the Etruscan Antiquities came from, though it appears he was less an academic more a chancer and a treasure hunter. I certainly couldn't find any precise records of his excavations and I made enquiries at the British Museum. I suppose I shouldn't say really, but they're quite keen to acquire a couple of pieces in the sale, particularly the Worcester replica of the oracle's bowl which Cornwallis commissioned. It's thought to be based on a lost original and no more are recorded, should smash the five thousand pounds estimate with any luck."

"Well, you're at the heart of the great and the good of the Auction world now Claire."

She was genuinely complimented by Harry's remarks but made light of it,

"You wouldn't have said that if you'd seen me traipsing through the dank old hall, struggling through cobwebs and mouse shit. Most of it was rotten of junk, we picked out these few treasures, thankfully the Waterhouse had been removed a while back or that might have rotted away. Yes the rest was pretty grim, so it's not all glamour."

"The rest?" asked Harry who was long enough in the trade to get excited about a house contents, even one that was half rotting and covered in mouse droppings.

"Yes all the broken bits and household always gets turned over to a local Auctioneers, the solicitors need us to clear the whole thing but no one's selling a broken fridge at King St." Claire laughed.

"So who is selling it all, has it gone?"

Claire walked back over to her desk and opened the drawer, sorting through a few notebooks.

"It's these chaps, Hyde and Barrel, livestock auctioneers. I think they cleared it all a couple of weeks ago, it should be going through their next chattels sale sometime this week. Nothing very exciting though, we've been through most of it and I promise there aren't any hidden gems, not Etruscan ones anyway."

Harry made a quick note on his phone of the auctioneers. He hadn't seen anything advertised and there was just a chance that they'd cleared the place out and were just going to offer it without any publicity or fanfare in a general sale. It would be ideal for a look through and there must he thought be something, knowing the provenance alone could make a fifty pound pine box worth a couple of hundred.

He thanked Claire for the catalogue and proceeded back downstairs, it was later than he'd liked and he knew he wasn't to get back home by five as he'd promised. On the way out he found Oliver coming in to view, he quickly pulled him to one side and showed him the Gervase Spencer clasp he'd found that morning at Grays. After a little too and fro with Oliver feigning disinterest but never actually letting the miniature out his grasp and a discussion about wether it was by Spencer or his pupil Spicer the second deal of the day was struck between the two men and another fifteen hundred pounds changed hands.

By now Harry was impossibly late and he called Bethan to tell her he'd see her around nine that evening and she shouldn't wait up if she was shattered, after all when you are a teacher, every night is a school night.

The next day Harry slept in, a bit shattered by the London trip the day before, Bethan had already got up and gone into school.

Having made himself a late breakfast he got out his phone to Google the livestock auctioneers, "Hyde and Barrel", even though they were local he'd never heard of them. They didn't have a website, encouraging he thought, but there was a phone number listed on a local directory site.

After giving them a quick call Harry found out their next general sale, which did indeed include the residual contents of Acton Hall, was only two days away and currently on view. They were only about a fifteen minute drive from his home on the outskirts of Bristol and near Acton Hall itself. Harry got himself dressed and ready and set off in the car, remembering the holy trinity of magnifying glass, torch and a working pen, essentials in any dealers "on the road" kit bag.

It was a pleasant enough day and the drive out was all verdant hedged country lanes and picturesque villages with the odd thatched cottage thrown in for good measure. Days like this made Harry glad he wasn't couped up in a small dark office in a major London saleroom as Claire evidently was, though he still wished it paid more.

When he arrived at Hyde and Barrel it was clear that the cattle side of the business was their bread and butter, everything smelt strongly of the "countryside" and the downstairs saleroom, just next to the rows and rows of outside metal stalls had the unmistakable smell of sheep.

"Catalogue please" he asked at reception.

"That'll be two pounds love." replied the portly middle aged lady who ran the office in a thick west country accent.

Harry handed over the two quid and got back a few photocopied sheets of A4 paper stapled loosely together at the corner. This was the sort of spit and sawdust auction that dealers dream of in their sleep, no Internet, no advertising and a catalogue a four year old could have written. He started to work through the room, top to bottom, end to end, looking under every table and in every box for the one possible thing Claire and her Christie's colleagues may have missed.

After a good two hours Harry could see Claire's assessment of the contents had been just about spot on, everything was either decaying or covered in the gently accrued layers of filth that only a hundred years of unthinking neglect could deposit. There was an ebonised side table, well, most of an ebonised side table, Harry had collected together a few spindles to the base which were lying around as parts of other lots, that might just be by Godwin. He'd bid on that, then there were two trays of Victorian costume and semi precious jewellery mixed in with odds and ends, scent bottles, snuff boxes, and little fragments and specimens from a collectors cabinet. There was also an old black and gilt japanned tin box, beautifully lettered in copperplate script "Mr Richard Cornwallis, Acton Hall" but it was locked shut and seemed to have something heavy inside, which sounded like builders rubble as he tilted it back and forth. He'd asked the lady at reception of they had a key or had tried to open it but he was only met with a vacant stare. He might have a go at that too, but he'd have to pay Gary the locksmith at least twenty to get it open and the same again for a working key. It hadn't quite been the treasure trove he'd hoped for, but it wasn't far and he'd come back tomorrow for the sale and see how his luck went on the Godwin style table.

On the drive back he passed by the turn for Acton Hall itself. He'd never seen it, despite being local and with nearly the whole afternoon still in hand and nowhere else to go, he took the short detour to his right and headed for the Hall. He could at least take a few photo's and show them to Bethan and the prospective purchaser of any of the items he might buy in tomorrow's sale.

After driving through a bit of thick woodland for about half a mile the road turned sharply to the right, it had narrowed down to only a single track with the odd worn out passing place on the side. Harry slowed quickly as he saw a small stone gatehouse perched on the apex of the turning, easy to sail past. Pulling onto the drive approaching the Hall which was only a short gravel track with cut lawns either side and the odd mature cypress and oak. There was a short ruddy faced man, in his mid sixties by the look of him in a heavy white shirt, armless leather coat, wearing cords held in place by a thick dark braces tending to some of the flower beds by the foot of the trees, Harry pulled over and rolled his window down,

"Afternoon, is it alright to go up and look at the Hall?"

The short, thick set figure turned and approached the open window.

"Afternoon, why would you be wanting to go up and see that dark old hole I wonder?"

"Hi, hello I'm Harry, I was just passing and had heard there was going to be a sale in London this week of some of the pieces from the house and thought it might be nice to call in and see it."

"Ahh you're one of them auction people are you."

The old man nodded as he leaned on the window of the car door drawing in closer to Harry.

"I'm Tom, not Old Tom mind, he was my father's father. I looks after the place at least till they've sold it but don't reckon no one's going to buy that dark old hole, not if they've the money to buys a nice house."

"So you've been here long, I mean your family, did they know the original owner? Mr Cornwallis wasn't it?"

"Derby Dick you mean?! Why yes my Great Grandfather worked here as a young footman for Derby Dick, earned himself a few quid too doing it. Look why don't you come for a cup of tea", Tom pointed to the stone gate house "and I'll show you"

Harry told Tom to get in to the car and he drove them back down the few hundred yards of the gravel drive to the small stone gatehouse which was Tom's home. He parked up and got out, admiring the gothic detailing of the pointed arch door and the narrow diamond glazed lancet windows.

"Pretty as a picture it is from the outside, true enough, but a right bugger to live in" replied Tom as both men slightly ducked their heads to get into the main small sitting room.

"Sit down, I'll just make the tea, whilst I do have a look at this."

Tom handled Harry a thick well worn family photo album which he'd just taken off a small oak dresser covered in Victorian pressed glass and Staffordshire flatbacks all resting upon lacework doilies.

He thumbed through front to back and saw Tom grow younger as he flipped back through the pages, then it was a figure who must have been Tom's father, then grandfather and then at the front of the album pictures of a young man in fine livery pictured outside the Hall with the other servants and the owner in the foreground with his wife.

"That's him" Tom came back into the sitting room with two heavily potted mugs brimming with dark builder's tea, "That's Derby Dick with my Great Grandfather, there, third along on the right, don't he look smart?"

"Yes, very" Harry replied "But why Derby Dick?"

"Ah, my great grandfather always took the mail to the village for posting and it became well known that Master Richard liked a gamble on the horses, some say its as how he made his fortune in the first place. Every week before the Derby my Great Grandfather would be back and forth with letters and parcels to the Post Office and all to bookmaker's across the country. It got that he took to looking in some of them and found the name of the horse that the Master was backing. That's how as this cottage ended up being mine, or at least my family's"

Harry just looked slightly puzzled at the old man. Tom could see he needed to explain it clearly.

"They all won."

"What?"

"Every horse he ever backed for the Derby, the all won, always. At first my Great Grandfather risked half a crown or so, but as two or three years passed he became so certain of it that he would bet a years wages on it, more sometimes if he could, yes if it had gone on for a bit longer we might have owned the big house too."

"Gone on?" Harry pressed him.

"Yes it wasn't long after that photograph was taken" Tom took the album from Harry and carefully eased the card sepia image from the four slip corners to turn it over,

"Yes here we are Spring 1890 tis the date, the year Derby Dick got married and it weren't three months later that he fell ill and died, just as great grandad was about to put a fortune he'd saved on the next race, shame."

"Do you know how he died, Derby Dick?"

"Fell from an upstairs window, one of the rooms at the very top of the house, a couple of the younger servants from the home and Mrs Cornwallis were witness to it, after that it all closed up and she left. Never sold it though, probably no need to and so we were just left here to keep an eye on the gloomy old place."

Harry now felt aggrieved he'd never passed this way before and met Tom when the house had still been full of its treasures, still all this history only added to his desire to buy something in the Hyde and Barrel general auction tomorrow, though it had gotten late again in his conversations with the old man.

"Thanks for the Tea and the Tales, it's late now but would it be ok to pop back another time, maybe next week and go up and see the Hall?"

"It'll be my pleasure if you knock on the gatehouse door I'll give you the keys and you can have a look round if you want to, mind you the place is near enough bare bones now and filthy as anyone's business, still if you've an interest."

"That'll be great thank you" Harry left in enough time to get home before Bethan and cook up a half decent dinner to make up in part for being back so late the night before from London and though he didn't quite admit it to himself, for being quite so pleased to have met Claire again.

The curry he'd made from found ingredients in the bottom of the fridge, including a slightly soft courgette and a half a red pepper once all the mould had been cut off combined with a mixture of cupboard spices and left over sauces to disguise any hint of sell by date cuisine. The table was laid with odd Victorian ironstone plates rescued from job lots, a Georgian glass carafe which was literally pences from a scout table top sale and two mismatched Georgian brass candlesticks which were cheaper than buying two plastic moulded ones from the supermarket.

"Brill, you've cooked" as Bethan closed the front door behind her, dropping her piles of marking in the hallway and throwing her handbag over the banister, she walked through to the kitchen where Harry had everything ready, he'd even bought wine and it wasn't yet the weekend.

"Good day? Shall I pour you a glass?"

"Please and no not really, Davy was misbehaving again, saw the Head again, we'll have to call in his foster parents for a meeting and see what we can do, I'm sure he's hyper or something. How was your day, was the sale any good?"

Harry lifted the pan of curry onto a mat on the centre of the table and got the rice which was keeping warm out of the oven.

"Yeah, couple of things, no treasure but I'll go back tomorrow and see how it goes. I did call into the Hall, didn't go in but met the caretaker, nice old guy called Tom and he's invited us back whenever."

"Us? You don't think you're dragging me round a dusty old Hall in my precious free time do you?!" Bethan exclaimed as

Harry put a playful arm around her waist and she spilt a little of the wine from her glass, laughing.

Harry was up early the next day and left Bethan sleeping, he wanted to be at the sale good and early to check everything one last time. As he pulled up to the livestock auction car park he saw at least two, no three, familiar dealers, one quite top end and worried that all his efforts might be wasted. They certainly were on the Godwin "style" side table, the pieces of which he'd gathered up around the saleroom which still smelt terribly of an uncooked lamb dinner. It was in for twenty pounds but the smarter dealer he'd seen sniffing round started straight in at "a hundred" for it to escalate in a matter of minutes upto four thousand. Harry was pleased his gut feeling that it might be by Godwin was right, but utterly gutted that everyone it seemed had found it, even though it was broken with at least two stretchers missing, it finally sold for just over eight thousand including the slap and he felt his day, his long day in the sheep shed, would be wasted.

After the excitement of the Godwin table a couple of the dealers he'd seen earlier left, they were clearly waiting to buy it for a few hundred as Harry had been but saw no reason to stay for the rest, in fact the room thinned out rather quickly and prices soon returned to five and ten pound bids. Well something is better than nothing Harry thought.

By the time it came to pay Harry had only spent a couple of hundred pounds but bought all three tray lots of miscellaneous jewellery, a nice if distressed Georgian walnut side chair on cabriole legs and just for good measure the old locked trunk which the auctioneer struggled to get a bid of a fiver for. He loaded up the car pleased with what he'd bought, so much so that he'd almost forgotten about the Godwin table.

That evening Bethan came back from the school to a more familiar scene than the thoughtfully prepared dinner the night before. Harry was sat cross legged on the sitting room floor surrounded by the boxes of "stuff" he'd just bought. Clean and dirty dusters and polishing cloths were strewn all around him together with match sticks, old tooth brushes and various tins of metal polishes and waxes. She could already see every finger on both of his hands were thick grey or black with tarnish and grime as he turned round and broadly smiled at her.

"I think I can tell but how was the auction babe?"

"Killed it. Apart from the table making eight grand, you know the one I liked, but all of this only cost a couple of hundred quid and look."

Harry had already cleaned up two nice silver commemorative medals, a pair of gold Victorian earrings, two small boxwood netsuke and a collection of neolithic or later arrow heads from the tray lots and he wasn't yet half way through. Bethan tried to look impressed but then Harry pulled out a long silver chain with a large pendant on the end.

"I couldn't see what this was, it was black and nearly took half an hour to clean, but look."

He handed it to Bethan, it was a thick long silver curb link chain, and on the end was a pendant of irregular form, about three inches long and as wide in places. After he had cleaned the blackened mount Harry had found a silver setting inscribed "Harriet Cornwallis, 1891" on the back and it was inset in the front with a large glazed pottery fragment decorated with a classical female head in blue and what appeared to be the beginnings of wings behind her, it was framed with seven cabochon blood red garnets.

"Oh it's lovely, so unusual" exclaimed Bethan.

"It's yours, no don't say no, I've more than covered my costs on the rest of it and will still make a good profit, look there's loads left to sort through"

Harry pointed to the two trays of odds and ends he still had to sort through and then, lifted his hand and pointed to the corner of the sitting room.

"Plus there could be a small fortune in that!"

It was the still unopened Toleware strong box inscribed for Richard Cornwallis.

"I've got to get it unlocked though I doubt its got anything valuable in it, but it only cost a fiver and once its empty its got to be a hundred, hundred and fifty unless its full of diamonds, but I'll sort it out at the weekend when I've got this lot here sorted cleaned and sold"

Harry kept on picking through the days haul, cleaning and where necessary gluing little pieces back together, by the time he'd finished that evening there was quite a respectable haul of Georgian and Victorian oddities, just the sort of thing which would fly out at the Bristol Sunday market and he could get a casual stall there for thirty five pounds. He'd deal with the box after that.

It was Friday and Harry was out and about the Cotswolds, viewing sales and popping into Antiques Centres, properly hustling to make ever more money, he never really stopped.

It had been an unexpected half day at the primary school Bethan taught at, a problem caused with the fire alarm system which was traced to the errant behaviour of young Davy which meant it closed at one and she had the afternoon at home.

She'd kept the pendant on for the last couple of days and really got to like it, everyone had commented on how unusual and striking it was, it was lovely of Harry to give it her, especially as she knew he could probably have sold it easily. It would be nice if she could do something for him, a surprise.

She cleared the kitchen table and went into the sitting room, lifting up the locked Toleware box, carrying it through and placing it on the table. She pulled up one of the kitchen chairs and laid out every small tool she could, a nail file, a couple of paper clips, a single hair slide with a thin metal clasp and a crochet hook that was in the sewing box for some odd reason. Like a surgeon preparing for a major operation she lined up the motley selection of instruments and began to operate on the lock. At first there was a lot of swearing and slipping, the lid had at least two fresh scratches on it, but if Bethan could control a class full of eight year olds she could certainly open a small brass lock. She started to get the feel of it and could hear things moving inside, the paper clips were twisted to fit around inside the lock and then, with two of them in she recklessly wriggled the end of the crochet hook around and heard "click", it was a miracle worthy of the old testament. She carefully took all the implements out and placed them on the table, then with both hands tentatively opened the lid, peering to see what was inside, hoping for Harry it might be something wonderful.

"Hi, I'm home, Bethan I'm back!" called Harry as he walked into the house that evening, the lights were on but there wasn't a reply and the TV wasn't on either, it was dead quiet, he walked through the empty living room and saw the box had been moved, he then walked through to the kitchen, again without a single sound, he opened the kitchen door slowly, worrying something might be wrong.

"What the hell are you doing?!"

"Shush, I'm nearly finished" replied Bethan, hunched over holding two pieces of pottery together, barely moving.

In front of her on the kitchen table was the now opened box and a series of thirty or so pottery fragments, mostly now rejoined thanks to a tube of super glue which Harry kept for repairs and a few hours of Bethan's time.

"Well they're back together now, look" she placed the two joined fragments of pottery she'd been holding together down on the table.

"What is all this?" said a slightly bewildered Harry as he slumped into one of the kitchen chairs.

"It was all inside the box, I managed to get it open this afternoon as I got sent home early and I found all these bits of pottery, brightly painted so I sat down and started putting them together, I've been at it for hours, its been quite fun. It looks like a large shallow bowl with mask handles by the look of it but I still can't really see what the scene is until I've got it all together but I think there might be one or two bits missing"

Harry looked at it all and remembered the Etruscan vases at Christie's that had been part of Cornwallis' early collecting and how Claire had said there was a lot of interest in them from the British Museum, he rushed into their bedroom to find the catalogue she'd given him and brought it back into the kitchen.

"Look, look, it might be one of these Bethan and if it is!"

They both sat as Harry flicked through the pages of the catalogue, they found the three large Krater vases but they were an entirely different shape to this bowl and though the decoration was similar it didn't look too much the same, so Harry's excitement declined a little.

Bethan knew how much Harry wanted to find that one thing which would pay off the mortgage and set them up for life, it had happened to dealers he knew which made it all the more harder, she could kick herself now for getting his hopes up.

"It's alright love, it was only a fiver and you've got the box open and whatever this is it's not complete anyway. We can take it down to the museum and see if it anything, don't worry about it not being like the ones in the catalogue"

She picked the catalogue up and took it back into the bedroom, thinking out of sight out of mind, but still kept leafing through, it was then she saw it and hurried back into the kitchen.

"It's Worcester, Royal Worcester and a good one is worth about five thousand."

Harry didn't turn round, he knew such a coarse pottery body had never been made at the Worcester factory.

"It's not love, it's a cheap Greek knock off made for gullible Victorian tourists, that's why they smashed the bloody thing"

"Look" Bethan insisted, now with the Christie's catalogue open and pointing to a lot on the page. Harry looked up to see a complete and perfect version of the bowl that lay in pieces on their kitchen table, he slowly and carefully read the catalogue description out loud.

"Lot 182, A Victorian large Worcester bowl, made c.1882 in the form of an Etruscan Oracle's bowl form the collections of Richard Cornwallis esq, (no longer extant)"

"Christ, this is it, this IS the bowl that they copied, the Etruscan one. hang on let's see what it made, I think Claire said the British Museum were interested in buying it"

"Claire? When did you see Claire?"

"Don't worry, just in London, she works there now" reassured Harry as he pulled his phone out his pocket and logged on to the Christie's website. He clicked through onto the Acton Hall sale catalogue and scrolled through the sale results as quickly as he could, 179, 180, 181, here 182 sold for"

He looked up at Bethan with his eyes wide and slowly said the amount

"Thirty eight thousand pounds, THIRTY EIGHT!"

"But there's was perfect wasn't it?"

"Yes, but that was just a copy, this I think is the real thing, God, look lets put it away safely for now and we'll get it off to a good restorer I know in the morning. See what she says, she's done lots of Museum conservation work and then I'll make some enquiries at the British Museum. Looks like I'm off to London again love, second time this week."

Early the next morning Harry had already been on the phone to Sarah asking if he could drop the pieces of the bowl off for restoration that day and please to do the work thoroughly, but quickly and that there would be a bonus in it for her. She agreed to him coming over and dropping it off straight away if he paid up front, which he was happy to do.

Next he was emailing Claire to ask if it had been the British Museum that had bought the bowl and that he may have some related ephemera that could be of interest, could she put him in touch with them for old time's sake? He was careful not to make any mention the broken fragments of what he hoped was a genuine Etruscan piece.

He got an email back about an hour later saying that it had been bought by a benefactor who was giving it to the museum and that she'd be going over herself at the end of next week to see the pieces were safely delivered. She'd have a word with the curator there but wouldn't make any promises.

After Harry had got dressed and dropped all the partially assembled fragments over to Sarah and given her five hundred pounds for a quick and thorough job he just had to wait in a state of electrostatic excitement, all the possibilities whirring around in his brain. It was a good job he had the Bristol Sunday market to focus on or he might just explode wondering if he had hit the jackpot after all.

Bethan manned the stall with Harry and it was just as well. The few cleaned up trays of curios he'd got from the Acton Hall sale flew out with people pushing in to rummage through and buy, after the first hour of the fair had finished, nearly all of it. Nothing quite so satisfying as selling out at a fair and it went a long way to distracting Harry from the bowl, that was until he got a text on his phone from Claire which read,

"Professor Lovell will see you tomorrow at the BM 11.00am SHARP, don't make me regret arranging it, he's a lovely old man but a bit dry and does go on, be nice. C x"

Harry quickly put the phone back in his pocket, he didn't want Bethan to see the small "x" at the end of the message, it was just Claire being polite after all.

Harry made the now familiar journey up to town and this time treated himself to a Taxi as he got out of the station which dropped him directly outside the British Museum. He made his way up the flights of steps and past the imposing portico, it had been an age since he had visited, and called into reception to say he had an appointment with Professor Lovell for eleven.

After a few minutes wait a short thin eccentrically bearded man appeared from one of the private side doors.

"Hello, I'm Jim Lovell, you must be Harry, Claire's chum"

"Yes hello, thank you for making the time to see me, I'm most grateful"

Harry said in his best ingratiating and grovelling tones.

"So it's the dear old Etruscans you want to know about"

"and the bowl you've acquired" Harry interrupted

"Yes, the bowls, come along with me I'll show you where they're going"

Professor Lovell lead Harry, surprisingly quickly for a man clearly in his seventies, down two or three corridors, up a flight of stairs and then through a small narrow service corridor which came out at the back of one of the galleries, in a small area which had been temporarily partitioned off from the public.

"What do you think?" asked the Professor

Harry looked around, there had been small room constructed with vibrant painted classical figures and mythical blue creatures on the walls. There were three plinths around each of the walls and a low table in the centre, all fitted with glass display case covers, though empty but with long labels attached to the base.

"It's a replica of the Tomba dei Demonii Azurri, excavated in Necropolis of Monterozzi, near Tarquinia in Italy, thought to date back to the fifth century"

"Yes, it's very nice, but what its got to do with the copy of the Etruscan bowl?"

"I've studied it for a long time now, since it was discovered back in 1985 and even went over myself, that's when I noticed the stone pillars that had been pushed over and crumbled, three of them and a low table. It was over there that I first came across Richard Cornwallis."

Professor Lovell could see he'd clearly peaked Harry's interest.

"He was paying for excavations on the same site in the early 1880's, though there was some unrest about not paying the local diggers on time, I know now he must have been down to his last few pounds. It was then that I think he unearthed a tomb very similar to this, but intact."

"Intact?" Harry queried.

"Yes, I think that originally these tombs were also used as temples to the spirits of the afterlife and were decorated with sacred vessels which would have sat on the fallen plinths which we've recreated here."

"That's why you wanted the replica Worcester bowl, for this display?"

"Yes that and the other three large Krater vases, Claire said you saw them at the auction. One decorated with a procession of children carrying votive offerings, the second with the priests at prayer or divination within the temple or tomb and the third decorated with the spirit of Charun, guarding passage into the underworld with his large hammer. We've previously found individual examples of all three, it was the Oracles bowl which we'd not seen before, none seem to survive though they are described in the historical texts. Sadly the Worcester reproduction was the nearest we could get."

"How do you know it's right then?" said Harry trying to bring the conversation around to anything Lovell had found out about it.

"I went up to the Worcester museum, they've got the full account of the order from Cornwallis in 1882, just a year after he'd come back from Italy, it clearly states it was a copy in fine porcelain of an original terracotta pot in the possession of Mr R.Cornwallis of Acton Hall, ordered at the sum of £28 and a small instruction that it was under no circumstances to be exhibited. Odd that, its quite a monumental piece, depicting the winged Goddess Vanth. It's possible that Cornwallis was familiar with the surviving Claudian accounts of the Etruscan divination ceremonies and didn't want the local gentry to think him pagan in his ways. He certainly did a lot in his later life to establish his good standing within the local community."

It was clear from the slightly glazed expression on Harry's face that Professor Lovell had slightly "left him behind" in the conversation, he suggested going to his office for a coffee and he'd explain it all a bit better. Harry gave a slightly bewildered nod and the old academic led him off through another series of service passages.

"Here we are, sit down" The room was bright and obviously at the rear of the Museum, all oak panelled with beautiful Victorian glazed bookcases and a fine Pugin looking desk with upholstered well worn green leather tub chairs, Harry could have made a cash offer for most of it as it stood.

"Here's the Claudian account of the divination ceremony"

Professor Lovell handed Harry a well worn worn penguin paperback book,

"You can borrow that if you like, but remember the Etruscans never really had a written history of their own, we rely a lot on what Roman Historians were writing a couple of hundred years later, largely influenced by rumour and bias, often painting the Etruscans as a blood thirsty lot of pagans which I doubt in truth they were.

Claudius recounts that one of the Roman Generals fighting the Etruscans sought to destroy their "sacred vessels" in the night so they could no more summon spirits up to foretell the course of battles the following day. It's probably superstitious nonsense, but their ridiculous belief in it may be why none of these Oracle bowls do survive. Certainly these Classical accounts would have been taken much more seriously in Cornwallis' time at the end of the nineteenth century. But even then we were turning to much more legitimate and scientific forms of archaeological research, thank goodness"

"Do you think Cornwallis did discover one of these bowls, an Oracle's bowl? In Italy?" Harry delicately probed again without revealing anything of his own hoped for discovery.

"Probably but it seems lost to us now. Cornwallis was an odd chap far less the serious academic much more the treasure hunter. I still couldn't find out how he'd paid the diggers and returned to England quite so well off, I suspect a little looting and selling of artefacts is behind it, though I recall that all the workers on his dig in the summer of 1881 were called away to look for a couple of children missing from the village, he may have taken the opportunity to leave then whilst they were all otherwise engaged.

I tried to find out everything I could for the notes on the

display on his later life. It appears he made his money fairly rapidly through the stock market upon his return to England but then diverted all his attentions to good works and furnishing Acton Hall. He set up the local foundling hospital a year later and latterly married the head Matron, Harriet Pinkney in 1890 who was a good fifteen years his junior. It was not long after that the accident occurred and the house and it's collections were shut up. It's been only recently that the charitable trust managing the estate ran low on funds and decided to dispose of all the remaining assets"

"Trust?"

"Yes set up by Harriet to care for children across the globe, its not well known but has given millions to worthy causes over the years, Harriet herself was a tireless campaigner after her husbands death and bankrupt herself in the service of the innocent, one of the reasons we didn't mind paying so much for the vases, it's all going to a good cause after all."

Harry picked up the book from the Professors desk and thanked him for all his assistance and said that if he did turn up any related ephemera from the few belongs he'd bought that the Museum would certainly have first refusal. He joked on the way out, as casually as he could, "and how much would you pay me for the Orcale's bowl if I found it?" The Professor chuckled back "oh one, two, three hundred thousand, so keep looking!" without a clue that it was currently being carefully pieced back together in a Bristol restorers workshop and that Harry was now headed off to collect it. Harry smiled.

On the quiet train journey back Harry read the book the Professor had given him, he became engrossed in the gruesome meticulous detail of the text, rituals described in minute detail by Claudius, he was still re-reading certain passages as the train came into his station, he pulled himself free of its darkness and got off, heading immediately to Sarah the restorers house to collect the bowl.

"Done" declared Sarah as Harry entered her small studio at the back of her Bristol terrace, converted garage with a roof light.

The bowl appeared in every detail to match the Worcester copy which had sold to the Museum, with one notable exception.

"Yes, I'm afraid you didn't have that bit" Sarah pointed to a unevenly shaped three inch hole in the base, just where the head of the Goddess Vanth should have been. Harry paused for moment in deep thought and said in an uncharacteristically low key voice,

"It's okay Sarah, do I owe you anything over the five hundred I left you?"

"No, it was easier to put together than I thought, that'll be fine. I'll just get a box and some tissue for you to take it back in."

Harry gingerly took the bowl into the back of the car and drove slowly back home, still very deep in the darkest of thoughts.

When Bethan got home that evening she was delighted to see Harry with the bowl all back together, the day had been manic. She told Harry how young Davy had hit another boy in her class and run off, the had to search the entire school and call in his foster parents again, it meant she had a mountain of marking to do this evening even though she knew they'd planned to go out.

Harry was very subdued about it all but listened intently, he seemed distant or perhaps troubled to Bethan but surely it had all been good news at the Museum? Harry excused himself as being very tired from the London trip and had an early night.

Bethan had stayed up till almost twelve marking and had slept in, the alarm hadn't gone off and Harry seemed to have got up early and gone out without telling her, he'd taken the bowl with him too. She tried calling his mobile a couple of times but it just went to voice mail.

She rushed to get ready and was quite put out when she couldn't find the pendant that Harry had given her the week before, she'd become really fond of it and hoped he hadn't had a change of heart and whipped it away to sell.

The day passed slowly enough for her, though her class were better behaved than usual, Davy's foster parents had clearly kept him at home today, perhaps to see the psychiatrist or doctor, especially after yesterday's misbehaviour. She was too relieved to complain or report it if they'd just decided to keep him home though, the break was too welcome for that.

That evening when she got home at a decent time she saw Harry sat watching the TV in the sitting room with the sound turned down in a bit of a daze, he looked frightened and as if he'd been crying, he was clutching a piece of paper tightly in his left hand and seemed unresponsive.

"What's the matter love? What's wrong?"

"It's the bowl" Harry barely turned his head or looked away from the TV as he gestured towards the kitchen,

"It works, the bowl works, that's how Cornwallis did it."

He started to tremble in his voice and swallow hard as another tear ran down his cheek, Bethan went in to hold him but noticed his arms and face had scratches, small scratches all over them, like he'd been in a struggle. Just then the TV announcer came on with the winning Euromillions numbers for that week, the jackpot had rolled over for a fourth successive time and was now nearly one hundred and forty million pounds. As they were drawn Harry looked blankly at the screen, now the tears, not of sadness but of guilt and regret washing over his face, before the final number had been announced he turned to Bethan and lifted up his left hand and gently whispered to her,

"We've won."

He then leant in towards her, cradling her head in his hands as he whispered, she pulled away but he kept talking, she pulled away again, more violently than before, horrified at what she had heard, she lifted up one of the brass candlesticks they had bought together when they first moved in and struck him hard across the temples, he slumped down into the chair, seemingly lifeless. Bethan ran out to get his tool box and entered the kitchen to fetch out the bowl.

The next morning two police cars were outside Harry and Bethan's house, police tape had been put around the perimeter of the front garden and a figure wearing a white hooded disposable cover and carrying a scene of crimes kit entered through the front door and called out

"Are you here too Geoff?" called out Toby, the senior of the two scene of crime officers

"Yeah, just for a couple of hours this morning to lend a hand getting it done but then we're all needed elsewhere."

"Where?" replied Toby

"Up by the woods near Acton Hall, they found that boy reported missing yesterday and it's pretty bad news, we need to do a finger tip of the surrounding area, but you and I just need to get this place sorted first before heading up. This shouldn't take too long though, just the usual domestic dispute gone wrong, husband and wife argued, she lost her temper and bashed him over the head with a candlestick..."

"Cluedo?!"

"Ha, bloody ha. Don't let the Super hear you say that. No she hit him with a candlestick, he's now in hospital in a coma and she's down the station being questioned. In a right state by all accounts. We're just here to record the scene in case he goes bad ways. I've just done the kitchen, found a burnt slip of paper in an ashtray already bagged up. There was a broken silver pendant in the bedroom, all twisted but the oddest thing is this lump hammer here in the living room and all these bits of pot."

Toby was curious about such a obvious weapon being right at the scene

"Wasn't this the weapon used then? Seems much handier than a candlestick?"

"Well just what I thought so I sprayed in with some luminol and put on the black light, that's the thing that's got me a bit puzzled."

"Well?"

"The hammer was clean, no traces of blood at all, just bits of clay and dust."

"That's not odd it just means she used the candlestick instead, actually did a Colonel Mustard in the Library"

"No, that's not it, the hammer was spotless but the luminol had also landed on the pottery shards surrounding it, they ALL fluoresced, nowhere else, but every pottery shard I tested fluoresced."

"Well, lets just bag it all up and send a piece off to be sampled, you never know we might get a match."

A Subtle Catch.

John heard the stable yard clock chiming one and rose from his desk in the estate room where he worked, overlooking the stable yard. He carefully placed the quill he was holding down on the polished pewter tray and closed the domed lid of the well.

The estate day book, which recorded any working incidents of note, deliveries and the weather reading for morning, noon and evening was carefully closed shut so not to blot the entries, then he lifted up the heavy oak slope of his desk and placed it carefully within.

He lifted his coat and hat from the ladder back chair beside him, the one Jones the estate carpenter had made from the felled Elm the year before and proceeded into the courtyard on a bright April afternoon. Two of the farm hands were loading up barrels of beer into a cart to take down to the workmen in the fields who were tending to the new spring lambs and the dairy maids were busy churning butter and making cheese for the week ahead. Jones was finishing repairs to one the estate gates on a makeshift hobby near a quiet light corner.

"Good afternoon Jones"

"Afternoon squire."

"Have you seen Samuel?"

Jones took a moment and placed down his draw plane amidst a pile of fresh sweet smelling wood shavings and straightened, lifting up a hand to keep the now high sun out from his eyes. He pointed upwards towards the woodlands bordering the nearby meadows.

"Was up by the woods last time I saw him, Squire Rawlings"

As if the boy had heard the two far off men talking he appeared running out of the woods, clutching a small pine box with a stiff leather strap that Jones had made for him as a present for his eleventh birthday.

"Father! Father!" he called out as he ran down the small meadowed slope towards Squire Rawlings and Jones stood in the rays of sunlight now flooding the red brick courtyard, casting an obelisk like shadow from the stable clock tower.

"Two new specimens and a mould I haven't seen before."

Samuel rushed to the feet of his father and opened the small pine box which had been fitted with three lift out trays of increasing depth. He lifted out the first with two butterflies upon it, one brilliant blue edged with black dots and the other a mottled tortoiseshell, beneath that was a tray holding a small knife, a polished reused spectacle lens mounted in a steamed and twisted piece of willow (again Jones' handiwork) and a small pencil and notepad, the final tray held a vivid yellow fungus bracket, the colour of thick custard.

"Well, you can keep the butterflies Samuel, but the chicken of the woods...",

His father the squire pointed to the large brackets of fungus, "that will be for our supper. When you go back to the house give it to Lucy in the kitchen and ask that she prepare it."

Samuel looked aggrieved, he had spent the best part of the morning climbing the tree, precariously reaching and cutting to get the specimen, now it was to be thoughtlessly surrendered to the cook. He deftly removed a small slice with his knife when no one was looking and placed it under his notepad.

The clock in courtyard chimed the half hour and the Squire turned to go back his office, he was expecting a visit from the Lord's agent and was discussing the lease of the other fields he had taken on the two years previous, before the crops had begun to fail.

Samuel ran back from the farm and stable buildings, rushing up to the small but well positioned Queen Anne brick manor house that his grandfather had built in 1707. He rushed through into his father's modest library and took down the glazed case where he kept all his choicest specimens.

There was a dried and mounted lizard he'd found a few years earlier, several butterflies and beetles, stuck on pins and some shells. It was his very own cabinet of curiosities, there were even small parts of a Roman vessel, red and decorated with figures and impressed with a partial name that one of the farm workers had unearthed sewing lasts years crops in the new fields. Whilst his father only had the meanest selection of books, some of which had been removed in the last few months, Samuel had made a point of reading every one. It had been the dearest wish of his mother before she died of pox when he was seven, that he might go on to one of the better schools and from there to Oxford, everyone agreed his bright and inquiring manner suited him for a life of study.

He pulled out the blue butterfly from his pine box and carefully placed it on a thick piece of card, from a collection of scraps he had saved and sorted by size and thickness. He took his finer knife and two long thin wooden utensils he'd whittled himself and manipulated the butterflies wings, delicately and gently until they were level and fully open. He took a small pin and secured it through the thorax, it was then gingerly placed into his small glazed museum.

He tided the tools away and took out the notepad and began to draw the butterfly and it's finer details in the book, noting where he had found it, at what time of day and the conditions of the weather. Just like his father, he was meticulous.

That evening, after some time spent reading familiar friends in the library he was called into dine with his father as had become their custom. With no other children in the house and with Samuel's father John steadfastly refusing to remarry, the two of them had formed a close and predictable routine.

Lucy came up from the kitchen, the staff had thinned a little in the last two years, to serve up dinner, the chicken of the woods, save for one small academic slither which had been saved beneath a notebook and a jugged Hare.

After grace had been said by his father Samuel took a small piece of each and a small mug of beer and began eating.

"Samuel, I need to have a serious word with you."

"What is it father?"

"I met with Lord Hargreaves land agent today, Mr Harker. They will not release me from the agreement to lease the additional fields, this and the poor harvests mean we must put considerable thought into your future."

"Am I not to go to Eton next year father?" the boy was perceptive enough, although he did not minutely understand the financial affairs of his father, to know that his future may not be the one he had hoped for. The old man paused a little, hesitant to break the news to the only light of his life.

"I'm afraid that we shall not be able to afford it Sam, it will need to be a trade for you, but the best trade that we can get. Your late mother's cousin, well second cousin is a Goldsmith in London. I have asked him by letter today for the terms by which you may be indentured to him as apprentice, able to learn a valuable trade and with time secure your own fortunes independent of my own."

"But father..." as soon as he began to speak the boy could see how hard it had been for his father to say that to him, he cut his words short and tried as best he might not to show the sadness in his face, he picked up the pistol gripped fork beside him and struggled down the small piece of Hare which was now skewered upon it's tines. The sadness of the situation, rather than the quality of the game made it a hard thing to swallow.

"Look Samuel"

his father began in an optimistic and gentle tone trying to raise his son's spirits, "you are so quick and dextrous with your hands you may go on to be the most acclaimed of Goldsmiths in the city, then, a gentleman of leisure you would be able to pursue all manner of pastimes, have a great and large library of your own, a room lined with specimens and cabinets"

It was unlikely, his late wife's cousin was only a buckle and box maker in Cheapside, Gutter Lane, far from the illustrious shops and manufactory's of Regent Street, but he felt if he gave some glimmer of hope to the boy he would feel better and make sending him away bearable.

Samuel made the most of the days he lad left on the small Shropshire estate with his father but it was scarcely a week before the reply arrived from his distant relation, James Eaton, that he would take Samuel as an apprentice for seven years for a nominal fee of fifty pounds. It was not a small sum but far less than the costs of sending Samuel to school, it would also be a trade that should set him up for life should things not improve on the estate.

A week later Samuel was packed and bound upon the Mail Coach for London and for the shop of his "Uncle James" as it was deemed most suitable to address him.

The Coach journey down was as miserable as you could imagine, no one taking real care of the boy, simply shoving him to pillar and post, and the carriage ride itself was most unpleasant on the uneven country roads. Respite only came in the numerous tavern stops and horse changeovers, from Shrewsbury where he had boarded they stopped first at Wolverhampton, then Birmingham and finally to London, the journey taking the better part of a day. He was greeted from the Coach by one of his Uncle's workmen, Taylor, he was a man in his late thirties, simply dressed in well worn clothes, thin and dreadfully pale, his hair was thinning and he wore spectacles,

he had a terrible hacking, persistent cough and stained finger
tips.

"You Sam?"

"Yes Sir."

"Don't be calling me Sir, I'm no Sir and have no want to be
either, just call me Taylor, Mr Taylor when your Uncle's in the
workshop and stay tight lipped. Don't talk unless you're asked
to and if you are answer quickly and to the point. Now grab
that trunk and we'll be away."

There was no cart and horse to greet him, Taylor, for all his
lean and hungry look was wirily strong, like thin wrought steel
and he held the handle of Samuel's small trunk and set off
down the streets at quite a pace, Sam held the back of trunk and
hurried behind, though Taylor was so fast the trunk kept
slipping and hitting the cobbled surface below. This continued
for a good half hour, weaving and pushing through busy side
streets all the time with Taylor rushing forward, only stopping
to hack up a thick piece of phlegm which was choking up his
lungs, thinking nothing of spitting it loudly into the street near
or upon any fine gentlemen that happened to have the
misfortune of looking away.

"Here we are"

They arrived at a small shop, a single bay window and door
which appeared to be lined with small display cases holding
small and delicate boxes, buckles, spectacle cases and other
novelties. Taylor pointed to the side street, narrow and after a
few steps crowded and filthy, a rat ran across Samuel's path but
he was too curious by the new and strange surroundings to

flinch back in alarm, instead he peered and studied everything he passed, from discarded square dark glass bottles, to the crates and bags of coke and coal around the workshop door.

"Go up into Mr Eaton's parlour, it's the first room up the workshop stairs, just above the shop, he's waiting for you."

Sam walked slowly up the twisting staircase, clutching the slender smooth wooden rail supported on its thin cast iron banisters. As he cleared the ground floor of the workshop he began to feel soft carpet beneath his feet and see the light coming from the row of small candles lining the corridor on slim mahogany side tables, he walked slowly down and paused at the first door on his left, he knocked lightly.

"Enter" came a dry stern voice from behind the door. He walked in to find a nicely if sparsely furnished room with a settee on splay feet in rosewood and a large centre table. The fire was lit and standing before it, dressed immaculately in a black suit was the bearded figure of his second or was it third cousin, not much more than thirty five years of age beside his two daughters Anne and Maria, with his wife Caroline seated behind them attending to some intricate needlepoint by the bright light of an impressive cast and gilt bronze Colza lamp

"Hello Uncle, I'm Samuel"

The man stepped forward and peered at the boy stooping down to meet his his eyes, fixing his gaze, merely an inch or two away from his face, his tone was low and steady, but insistent.

"I've been paid fifty pounds, that's all, by you father to teach you all I know about this trade, quite the bargain you understand. So much so that I shall expect you to do double your share of the work, I have had apprentices indentured to me for eighty and a hundred pounds, so you shall have to match their purses with your labour."

He rose and stiffened again,

"and please to call me Sir within the workshop and Mr Eaton if you are called to see me in the shop, though that will not be for some time yet. Anne will show you where you sleep tonight."

Eaton's youngest daughter Anne, perhaps only a year younger than Samuel took up one of the round silver chambersticks chased with a border of flowers in the main room and proceeded to light it from a spill from out of the Davenport porcelain vase upon the chimney piece. Once lit she motioned, silently, for Samuel to follow her. He stopped at the door and turned to his Uncle and said a simple "Thank you" , Eaton did not acknowledge it.

They proceeded down the main carpeted corridor once more and met a small door at the end, once opened it led up a smaller wooden staircase to the household servants quarters. Anne led him through to a small Attic room at the end of the narrow corridor. It had a small, unlit fireplace with no scuttle or coal, a narrow old bed and a small simple pine chest with a dented brass chamberstick, lacking any candle and a chipped enamel tin bowl and a jug resting upon it. The only light in the room, except from Anne's candle was the six paned sky light. He could also just make his trunk which Taylor must have brought up in the far corner.

Anne wasn't unfriendly or unkind towards Samuel, though she was clearly nervous, possibly of doing the wrong thing so was quite perfunctory with her instructions to him,

"Father says this will be your room. You are to rise with the other household servants at six, be sure to go and wash and dress and then eat with them. Afterwards go down to the workshop where Father will instruct you with your daily duties."

"Thank you." replied Samuel. As Anne turned to leave she took out a small candle stub she had slipped into her pocket downstairs whilst her father had been addressing Samuel, she placed it into the battered brass sconce of the chamberstick on the pine chest and lit from the one she was carrying, turning to say "Goodnight" at the door. There were certainly a kindness in Anne that she had not inherited from her father or her mother.

Alone, Sam picked up the chamberstick and surveyed what would be his new home for possibly the next seven years, the term of his apprenticeship. The room was bare and uncleaned, suddenly something like a small beetle scuttled along the boards, Sam moved quickly to trap it in his hands and placed it into the jug on the chest.

He went and opened his trunk, digging beneath his clothes and few books to retrieve the small pine specimen box Jones had made for him. He opened it and took out the top two trays to get to the tools below, his small knife, magnifier and a selection of pins and cards.

He made his way back over to the chest with the now dwindling light from the chamberstick being helped by three or four bright rays of moonlight coming from above, now some passing clouds had been blown away. Arranging the knife, pins and card in a straight row, he tipped the jug into the bowl and the large beetle, in fact a cockroach fell into it, he grabbed it lightly and quickly with his hand and inserted the tip of the blade deftly between the lines of its carapace, piercing it above the thorax and rendering it lifeless.

He took the lens and held it up to his eye, he was not revolted by it but wondered at the minute and clever function of the creature, it's hard complex parts, all beautifully articulated. It was placed on a suitable piece of card and pierced into place with thin steel pin. The stub of the candle was flickering and guttering badly now and he decided to place his first London specimen in the drawer of the chest, deciding to finish the mounting in daylight.

Doing what he had done so many times before in the sunlit fields and woods of his home in Shropshire gave him a definite sense of comfort that had previously eluded him since his arrival this bustling unfamiliar and slightly frightening city.

The next morning Samuel rose and ate with the three household staff, cook, footman and maid, they barely spoke to him and were all surly in their demeanour, making him sit apart from them at the table and giving him a small bowl of thick cold porridge before shooing him down into the workshop.

It was already busy with hammering and hot with lit kiln and brazier as he made his way down the winding stair to the workshop. His Uncle, his Master, Mr Eaton, was stood waiting for him, clearly perturbed at not being in the comfort of the sitting room or in the shop front with the customers.

"Here!" he shouted pointing to the floor in front of him,

Samuel ran and stood to attention. Eaton grabbed him firmly by both shoulders and span him round.

"This is where you'll learn your trade, Mr Taylor who met you yesterday is in charge of this workshop. You will do everything that Mr Taylor asks you to and if you are diligent and work hard there should be no cause to meet with the stick."

Eaton pointed to a hard thick piece of bramble hanging near the workshop door, braced with blackened wire in places where it had nearly given way through the severity of the beating it administered.

"I shall be in the shop, upstairs with Mrs Eaton or out on business"

As Eaton said "business" Taylor looked up from his bench across to Frenchie with a look of sheer disbelief that made the two men briefly smile. Eaton continued,

"but if you should hear this bell, attend to it. I or my wife may need you to do an errand in the City for us, there's no sense sending a skilled worker from his bench now that you are here. You will work Monday to Saturday morning and at any other times if required, Sundays will be your own. I have not great care for the organised religion"

Taylor looked up and smiled at Frenchie again, who quietly chuckled,

"though my wife and daughters attend church, you will not be obliged to go with them, indeed I should prefer it if you did not."

"Yes Sir" replied Samuel. As Eaton walked off up the stairs to begin the days strenuous relaxing.

"Right" said Taylor, "I better shows you who we are and what we do"

The workshop was a large rectangular room, Taylor himself sat at the main large oak bench at the centre of the room, used for casting, filing and finishing their mainstay of buckles and tongs. Frenchie was the next most senior worker and sat over in the far corner next to the largest and brightest of the workshop windows. He had been a prisoner of war but had secured his freedom through amassing a small fortune in making ingenious mechanical toys from the animal bones at the prison camp he was confined in, being allowed to sell them to visitors in the local area, giving almost all of it over to the guards to secure his lawful release.

He had fallen into military service through misadventure rather than conviction in France, being something of an old Royalist at heart, so had preferred to stay in England and travel down to London to find a job in his old profession as a Goldsmith. The strong anti french feeling had meant that he did not secure the position which his skills deserved, though Mr Eaton, ever the hungry wolf, spied an opportunity and indentured him at half the going rate for a worker of his skills.

His work was to finish some of the fine gold boxes and buckles which Eaton supplied to other large companies, never selling them in his own shop. Frenchie often said he had worked under Ducrollay, then Biennais in Paris and made works for the King himself, even to the point that he had fashioned a small gold milk pail scent for Marie Antoinette that had been a favourite of hers, hanging around her neck and laying upon her breast, that was a story everyone had heard at least once, but his skills at the bench certainly testified that those stories may well have been true. He finished the most meticulous goldwork, sometimes in two of three colours of gold that he would specially make up with various secret metallic additions. His work had been supplied through Eaton to both to Rundells and Green Ward and Green, both Goldsmiths to the Crown.

At the other side of the shop was "Tonks" he was a very different character, quiet and morose, though understandably so. He did all of the polishing and gilding work in the shop, his most striking feature was the small leather patch tied across his cheek and nose. Sam learnt from Taylor that gilding was a well paid but hazardous process. Gold would be mixed to a paste with mercury, that would the be applied to the object you wanted gilded and the mercury burnt off in a kiln, leaving a thick lustrous layer of gold behind. Unfortunately the mercury vapours were inhaled by the gilders causing madness and illness, in Tonks case he had done it for two years before the soft tissue of his nose and cheek had begun to deteriorate, hence the leather patch to conceal the disfigurement. He had left the large gilding workshop riddled with fumes, though scarred for life and come to Eaton, as Frenchie had, at an advantageous rate. It did at least relieve him of a constant risk and hazard, he did only two or three days gilding a month at best now.

Taylor for his own part had just been a good workman for the master to whom Eaton himself had been apprenticed, John Summers. He had seen for himself Eaton do little or no work other than to attend to his master's only daughter, who was now his wife, sat embroidering upstairs in the room above them. By the time Summers died, Taylor was running the day

192

to day business of the workshop single handed, but lacked the education, ambition or nerve to set up on his own account.

Taylor sat down at his bench and hacked up another gobbet of phlegm, hurling it into the large brass spitoon beside him, he wiped his lips with a thin grey cloth from his pocket and continued addressing Samuel in his duties.

"Fetch and carry, take messages, sweep and clean the shop, tidy all away that I tells you and when that's done come and keep a keen eye on the work we do. If your quick in your wits you'll pick this up in a year or two and as you grow you'll do more. Pay most attention to Frenchie's work when you can, I've not seen a finer worker in all my time in the trade, and stay clear of Tonks if he ever starts to mumble to himself, the vapours made him wicked quick to temper. Right now start as you mean to go on and take that besom and clear the workshop floor."

Samuel took the broom from up against the wall and as was his nature began a very ordered sweeping of the workshop floor, along the length of each wooden board, back to front, moving and placing back any obstacle in his way. By the time he had finished amid the hammering, roar and heat of the kilns and braziers, he had three neat piles which he was about to brush out into the street.

"No!" called out Taylor, pointing to a large iron scuttle next to the door.

"All the sweeping go in there, they're collected every week by the refiners."

Samuel looked puzzled.

"We works in gold and silver don't we? Filing off and graving the precious metal? Well where do you thinks all those bits goes?"

Taylor stamped on the floor as he bent forward and coughed again to clear his throat.

"It's all there, mixed in with the muck and grime of the floor, flecks and grains of silver and gold. The refiner takes them and melts it all down in a far larger furnace than we has 'ere and pays Mr Eaton so for the privilege. There's money in muck young Sam and don't you forget it."

The rest of the day Sam, as he was now called by everyone in the workshop, had swept, cleaned, washed, scrubbed nearly every surface that he could. Even when one task had been finished he was eager to begin another, not impatient, just industrious. By the end of his first week he had become of genuine use, not just from his work ethic but because he was so quick to learn. None of the workmen needed to tell him anything twice and it was often the case that he would learn a new skill simply by observation, his eyes drank up every motion and technique they saw. In the evenings, he would pick up some of the workshop rubbish and even begin to fashion small things for himself.

Two thin waste edges of steel cut out from the stampings of the chapes for the buckles were carefully tucked into the pocket of his small leather work apron. In the evening, cleaning and sorting the tools and benches for the men, he had about half an hour on his own to do some little bits of work, as long as they were not loud enough to disturb Mr Eaton in his sitting room above.

He gently hammered out the two strips of metal, each to a fine point and scored them deeply on one side with a file, the next day he took them out and soldered the flat ends together, polishing and burnishing the join when it had cooled. By the end of the week he had added a fine long pair of steel tweezers to add to the other items in the bottom tray of his pine specimen box from home.

It was a week or two later that through his industry and a growing trust in his ability that Sam began to be asked to deliver orders to nearby customers and take parcels of the partially finished silver components for assay at the nearby Goldsmiths Hall.

Each and every part of silver had to be submitted at the Hall in the registered Silversmiths name, small scrapings would be taken to determine the quality of the silver was up to standard and the duty, now a shilling per ounce paid and the appropriate marks struck upon as a receipt.

Sam began to notice that when Taylor had cast and partially finished a large batch of shoe buckles, perhaps thirty pairs, he was only ever sent with a dozen or so of the smaller ones to the Assay Office, the others being placed in a box beside Taylor who would always say that he'd deal with them directly, yet he never, as far as Sam saw left the workshop. Still they were finished and fitted with the rest and went off, perhaps to another silversmith to have marked he thought, it was certainly a trade where some pieces could be supplied "in the white" (unmarked).

Sam was allowed to write to his father in Shropshire every month, but he did so in the sitting room of Mr Eaton and under his full and watchful eye. Sam knew enough to know that his correspondence would be gone through, before posting so he kept his notes affectionate and optimistic, it was also the case that he did not want to be a source of worry. He could not write in private or post a letter out as the allowance agreed between his father and Mr Eaton of some four shillings weekly was never paid nor indeed ever mentioned by Mr Eaton beyond the day that Samuel had asked for two shillings to purchase a small pad and some pencils when those he had ran out.

Eaton exploded with rage at the suggestion and recalled how the fifty pound settlement for taking him as an apprentice was a paltry sum and done only to assist a distant relation in need. Eaton knew how to express himself in the cruellest terms possible when the need arose. It was for Samuel "to repay the debt by his good and earnest labours and should not seek recompense for his efforts". Samuel, ever calm and now accustomed to the ways of 26 Gutter Lane, knew full well he would indeed endeavour to repay the debts accrued though he felt they were not financial ones.

Things carried on with a now familiar routine. Though Sam was indeed yearning for the sun lit fields he'd left behind, he was also fascinated in his new environs. Saturday afternoons and Sundays were for the most part, unless an urgent order needed to be delivered, his. He would explore the surrounding streets and buildings, drawing up his own map and finding delights in pursuing specimens for his growing cabinet of curiosities. Sometimes he would venture down to the river and had befriended one or two of the Mudlarks that plied their trade, often exchanging small things he had made with cast off pieces in the workshop for a stone arrow head, or a small fragment of broken pot, or particular interest would be any small insect or creature that had travelled aboard one of the ships which were frequently unloading, after six months he had an impressive variety of beetles and odd shells and was familiar to many in his search for the city's unwanted curiosities.

It was around that time that there was a commotion at the shop. About eight in the morning Wardens of the Goldsmiths company knocked at the door to inspect the premises, they had been told counterfeit wares were being sold. Taylor, upon hearing them arrived moved the large brass half full spitoon beside his desk and pushed up two clear loose boards, he took a leather bag from the drawer of his bench and thrust it in, nailing the board down quickly and placing the spitoon back in it's place. Everyone then carried on as usual as the Wardens made a search of the premises and examined in detail all the finished and part worked up goods in the shop. Two or three pieces were taken away for further examination, but the ease and politeness with which they were surrendered showed that nothing would prove to be amiss. The spitoon was never touched.

That evening Taylor took Sam to one side and explained, calmly what the boy had seen him to do that morning.

"Now you've been ere long enough to know the master and his ways, I mean his thrift."

"Yes Taylor."

"Well, now with duty on silver being a shilling and ounce and some of these buckles so large, as much as three or four ounces a pair there's a good profit to be made by any man that dares to put his own mark on em, rather than that of the Hall. Frenchie being so skilled and a prisoner of late was asked you see to do a job of work by Mr Eaton and he didn't ave much say about it."

Taylor pulled out the small leather bag he had earlier hidden beneath the spittoon. It contained four or five long steel punches, each had been engraved, by Frenchie with a very passable impression of the Assay Office's mark for silver, a lion and the King's head to show the duty has been paid.

"If we're careful as how we marks em there can be upwards of one of two hundred pairs marked this way, now you can do the adding up of that at a whole silver shilling an ounce. Now you must keep all of this strict quiet to yourself or its the gallows or transportation for us all."

Sam had never seen a kangaroo, that was his first thought, but he knew any delight he might have of being free of Mr Eaton would be short lived, he did not wish that the rest of the household should suffer, he swore then and there never to disclose it, but inwardly also made a pledge to benefit from it himself.

Sam did however realise that as the batches of larger buckles were not being marked at Goldsmiths Hall they were not being assayed either. This meant if a small proportion of the silver used to make each batch of castings was substituted with copper no one would readily detect it, not if it was small enough.

The skill would be in getting the copper and replacing the silver, but he was already trusted with loading up the crucible for the weekly casting when Taylor had readied the moulds.

When Sam cleared up the workshop and gathering the daily sweepings he would pull out any small parts of copper wire or sheet that might be used in making the cheaper gilded buckles which Eaton also supplied to some of his lower end customers. Ingeniously Sam even fashioned his own small balance from a length of steel and a small weight which would tip at exactly the amount of the small ingots of silver bought in which were used, six ounces. So when the larger silver buckles were to be cast he would place exactly six ounces of the copper trimmings when he had them in the crucible and load up the silver ingots above it, carefully taking one for himself, the resultant alloy would only be a little under the sterling standard and no one in the workshop it appeared, was any the wiser when working and finishing the cast buckles from it. Finally Sam had secured a small income of his own.

He could not obviously spend it without raising questions, but it did seem that his pencil for note taking never shortened and the last page in his notebook was eternally blank. He had taken a tip from Taylor and loosened a board in his own small room, improving enormously on the design by fashioning a crude hinge to secure one end and an invisible catch, worked by means of a thin wire attached to a knot in the wood of the board beside it which could be removed to secure or open it, it was ingenious.

Frenchie had observed the boy's growing ingenuity. Whilst Sam was content to help Taylor finish a fine openwork pair of shoe buckles, with the series of files and punches he used to bring the decoration alive, he was almost bewitched with

Frenchie's ballet like elegance, when his fingers danced over the surface of a plain piece of metal, transforming it.

Frenchie could pick out figures and birds, beautiful flowers with a few deft turns of his graver, or more laboriously tapping out a fine scene in three colours of gold upon a small black ground of pitch to save the delicate sheet from splitting. Most of all he loved the small automaton that Frenchie might combine into a snuff box. Sam was sent from time to time to get small parcels from a Mr Vulliamy in Pall Mall, Frenchie would say "he is a genius with a spring, I with a graver, together we can make the most beautiful things".

It was true that on occasion Frenchie would be asked to make some fine gold parts for Vulliamy's watches, whereas he would supply the movements, drawn to a particular design, for inclusion in some of the finest gold snuff boxes that Frenchie made.

As time passed things carried on much as they had with Sam working in the shop, training in more and more complicated tasks, beginning even to assist Frenchie in some of the most delicate work. Eaton continued to be stern and largely absent from the day to day running of the shop and Anne his youngest daughter was growing up to be quite a beautiful young woman, much to the increasing attention of the busy but largely lonely Samuel.

It was five years into his apprenticeship that the first tragedy was to upset the stable environs of Gutter Lane, firstly Mrs Eaton, a stern and largely responsible figure to whom the business had actually passed upon her father's death died herself from a case of Cholera which had effected many locally.

Although Samuel hadn't realised it, she, acting through Mr Eaton had been the steadying hand upon the business and its proper running, after her death Eaton made little pretence of respectability and was out most evenings drinking or "amusing" himself in local brothels, leaving the running of the shop to Taylor, who's cough was only worsening. Sam helped as much as he could to keep things going. Also after her mother's death Anne returned from her boarding school, Sam had only ever seen her briefly in the Summers and at Christmas, but she had now returned full time to take her mothers place in running the day to day needs of the household as her older sister Maria had already been married off.

Sam was pleased at first to have her back in the house, he still fondly remembered how she had had the kindness of thought to give him that candle stub his first evening in the unfamiliar house which was to become his second home. He was less pleased to hear the drunken shouting and crying that began to fill the house, two of the household staff were dismissed in bouts of anger by Eaton with Anne having to adopt many of the duties of a maid.

Sam did his best to comfort Anne when he could with a kind word or a small gift made in the workshop below in his own time, left for her in the evenings by the door of her room, but he seldom saw her without her father a looming presence in the room.

As for the workshop it seemed to have lost the discipline and direction it once had, he no longer felt the camaraderie amongst the men working there, again he longed to return to the fields of Shropshire where his father had just been managing to keep the estate running, though at the cost of most of the furnishings within the house and all but one of it's staff.

It was then that the second misfortune was to befall the small workshop in Gutter Lane. Once more the Wardens of the Company visited unexpectedly to search the premises looking for counterfeit punches. Sadly with the disarray within the workshop and Taylor's failing health the small leather pouch containing the counterfeit punches was discovered, Mr Eaton was called down to be questioned about the matter.

I the deftest piece of lying Samuel had ever seen, Eaton decried any part of the offence and immediately pointed it as an abuse of his kindness in offering to employ a former prisoner of war, directly pointing the finger of blame on Frenchie, he was immediately arrested and taken to prison whilst the Wardens continued their investigations.

Sam spent that night, the worst of his life this far listening to Anne being mistreated by her father as his dear friend was awaiting trial in jail, with Eaton his direct accuser. He might, if any other young man, have run away, back home, or sobbed into his thin cotton pillow.

Samuel lent down by the floor boards and lifted the loose fitted knot of wood free, pulling the wire which released the compartment he had made. He withdrew his childhood pine specimen box and took out the notepad and pencil. He lit a candle, counted out the money he had saved over the years, some twelve pounds and began to draw designs and complications in the pad for a snuff box, similar to the ones Frenchie had shown him how to make.

The next morning, with the workshop in disarray and Eaton barely sober Samuel presented himself to his distant relation and master.

"Mr Eaton, I would very much like to take up the work of Frenchie now he is awaiting trial in jail."

The sore headed Eaton snorted disdain at the suggestion,

"You're no match for Pierre, he was one of the best workmen I've had and you've barely completed your apprenticeship"

Sam was unshaken and had expected this.

"Then allow me to fashion a box, a presentation piece, a snuff box to you Sir as proof of my ability, in silver with gilt parts and as fine as any work that Frenchie did, even with a small automaton within if you'd allow"

Normally Eaton would continue to mock the boy and send him on his way with a swing or two from the bramble switch, but he knew there were orders, valuable orders waiting that only Frenchie had the skill to complete and despite everything he was aware of Sam's abilities, but still not absolutely sure, might the boy be that skilled?

"One opportunity for you, a fine box and just two weeks to make it. You will use only silver and get Tonks to gild any parts that may otherwise be of gold, but you will be liable for all the cost of it should it prove a waste of my time and metal."

Sam nodded but asked one more thing

"and may I go to Mr Vulliamy and ask for the mechanism as Frenchie did?"

"If he agrees to it I see no reason why not, but this is all your responsibility and this box will need to be your masterpiece."

Eaton returned to the sofa in the sitting room and slipped the stopper from a decanter of port at half past nine in the morning.

Sam entered the workshop to find both Taylor and Tonks morose and dispirited at Frenchie's arrest, with no more love for Mr Eaton as Sam had himself, though they spoke of it freely now.

"He's a bad one right enough, I know we was all involved but to turn on Frenchie like that, it's just not right" Taylor moaned, bent forward over his bench, kicking the leg with his stiff old boot in anger.

"Taylor, Tonks, I've asked Mr Eaton if I may replace Frenchie at his bench."

The two men looked fit to burst when the boy spoke out, but he raised his hand to placate them,

"If you will aid me in the next two weeks to complete my masterpiece we may do better for ourselves and our friends, will you trust me?"

Both men had known Sam long enough to trust the young man and agreed to do what he asked, when he asked, without further question.

Sam set to work at the bench, the box he was to make, the box he had designed, would be engine turned on all sides but with an elaborate heavy cast thumbpiece of flowers and acorns. The cover would have a double hinge, lifting to reveal the interior box as normal but also hinged to show an automaton scene concealed within the deep double walled lid which would operate upon pressing a small concealed catch. The scene he decided upon was one close to his heart, all manner of small creatures, butterflies, beetles that would move or beat their wings, they would he'd decided be bordered by a serpent which when operated would encircle the border of the box with a to and fro motion. Each of the separate sections would be wrought, engraved and gilt to give the imitation of the snake's skin moving, he would even model the head with two small fangs. He had seen Frenchie make something similar just with butterflies some years earlier and was familiar with the workings needed to drive the action, though he had made a small modification of his own.

Work progressed well and Mr Vulliamy agreed to assemble the simple variant movement within the time Sam had been given for an apprentice of his old friend, he had also offered to speak in favour of Frenchie at his trail and in the absence of Mr Eaton's damning testimony that might be enough to save him from the charge.

Samuel began his work in earnest on the box to the exclusion of everything else, except for Sunday's when he went out and made numerous urgent enquiries amongst those he knew on the river for particular specimens, offering twenty shillings to anyone who could find it.

Towards the end of the second week the box had been

assembled and finished to the highest standard that he could, the automaton movement of several gilt and frosted silver Butterflies whose wings trembled as the clockwork movement drove into motion. Then there were the Stag Beetles that scuttled and turned on spindles as their jaws opened and closed and his most ambitious detail realised, a serpent that moved around a channel specially cut into the edge of the inner lid, which rippled gently back and forth as it moved, faithfully imitating it's natural motion.

 All Sam needed to do was finish the catch on the inside which when depressed and held would set the clockwork movement in motion. He took the small plain silver button and began to smooth and engrave it with a flower head, small punches in the middle for the stamens, he pierced one small hole. He spent that evening in the meticulous finishing of it. He wound the movement and tested it once, placing his thumb briefly in his mouth. He then opened up the specimen box and removed something from the lower tray from a small glass jar. Afterwards he reset the mechanism, all ready to show it to Eaton the next morning.

The next day he rose early and dressed, it was the day he would present his "masterpiece" to Mr Eaton, He placed the box on one of the small felt lined trays from the shop and waited patiently outside the door of the sitting room, waiting to be summoned in.

Eaton opened the door and showed Sam to the table and pointed for him to place the box down for inspection. Eaton sat as Sam stood upright without uttering a word, though his eyes darted too and fro from the box to Eaton's face.

It appeared to Eaton a very well made box, well finished and as elaborate as some of Frenchie's work. He opened it by the thick cast thumbpiece and saw the plain gilt interior,

"I thought it was supposed to have a movement?" he snapped.

"It does here, in a concealed cover." Sam pointed to a small lip beneath the heavy thumbpiece, Eaton opened it with ease, the whole thing being so well and smoothly fitted together.

"My word!" he was taken with the unusual tableau of creatures in silver and in gilt all against a ground of grasses and flowers, like a summer meadow near a stable yard.

"How do you make it go?" he inquired, now genuinely excited to see it work.

"Just this button here." pointed Sam without touching it

"But I did not have time to fashion a stop/go, you must hold it lightly down to keep it running"

Eaton pressed and held the small round foliate engraved button as the scene enacted its motion. He saw the butterflies flap their wings, the beetles dance and the serpent slither around the edge of the lid.

He did not, could not see the small fine chains of the movement inside also winding around a barrel which pulled a hair's breadth tensioned metal wire to release a small sprung catch that held back an impossibly thin small blued steel needle, propelling it up through a near invisible hole made in the dead centre of the flower engraved button he was holding down.

Eaton barely felt the small sting in his thumb as the blued steel pierced his flesh and then seamlessly retracted, though he did place the box down to see a small bead of blood had appeared on his thumb as he placed it briefly to his lips to soothe it.

"Sorry I must not have filed off every sprue of the engraving" said Sam as Eaton lurched forward, upsetting the table and collapsing on the floor.

He began briefly choking, his hands grasped around his throat, Sam stepped back and did not speak or move except to retrieve the box. He'd been told countless times by Eaton to stand silent in his presence unless otherwise instructed to do so and Eaton was in no position to instruct him.

It was a bright Summer morning and Mr Samuel rose from his late father's desk in the estate room facing out into the stable yard, as the clock chimed one. He took up his coat from the elm chair and walked out, he saw Old Jones working on a broken scythe handle.

"Have you seen young John, Jones?"

"Why he's up in the woods Master Samuel."

As the young boy ran down towards the two men across the meadows.

"Father look" John carried the familiar well worn pine specimen box that Jones had made for him as a boy all those years ago.

"Come on John, your mother will be waiting for us in the house, you can show me what wonders you've found in the woodland there."

As they got to the Hall Samuel asked Lucy the maid where his wife Anne was, she told him she was writing in the library. The father and son entered the oak lined room which was fitted at every opportunity with high bookcases fully stacked with all manner of books on natural history, geology, chemistry and every other subject of modern thinking that you could wish to name. Beneath each bookcase was a bank of fine rosewood specimen drawers and range of glass display cases, all fitted and lined containing examples of shells and creatures from every part of the world, all collected by Samuel much to the delight of his son who shared his passion.

In one case alone stood a small finely turned silver snuff box, with a thick heavy thumbpiece. Encircling it was a preserved specimen of a south sea serpent, a very rare specimen that Samuel had acquired in London as a young apprentice for the not inconsiderable sum of twenty shillings.

Young John was as ever fascinated by it and wanted to get it out but the case which was firmly and securely locked.

"Why do you always keep the snake locked away?" said the inquisitive young boy looking up at his father.

"It's beautiful John but it's very deadly too, I keep it locked so no one I love will ever hurt themselves upon it."

"But if it's so dangerous why keep it at all?"

"Two reasons John, firstly because it is a rare and beautiful specimen, it's not to blame for being deadly, it is simply it's nature, how it was made to protect itself by God and secondly it still serves to protect my little masterpiece that was the start of all that's good and precious in my life, though it is no where dear to me as you"

He picked the boy up and kissed him on the cheek, turning to smile at his beloved Anne who was at the desk writing a short note to Master Taylor, to thank him for the continued profitable running of her late father's workshop in Cheapside.